STORM COUNTRY

The Anthology

SEVENTY SHORT STORIES AND POEMS

MISSOURI WRITERS' GUILD

www.MozarkPress.com

Copyright © 2011

Mozark Press LLC, Publisher
PO Box 1746, Sedalia, Missouri, 65302

Publisher's website: www.Mozarkpress.com

Cover Picture: Used by permission, John Hacker
Cover design and book layout by H. Ream.

ISBN: 978-0-9844385-4-9

DEDICATION

This anthology is dedicated to the past, present and future students and librarians of the Joplin School District.

Cover photo: Used by permission, John Hacker
Joplin Project Organizer and Coordinator: Claudia Mundell,
President, Joplin Writers Guild

Publication made possible through contributions by Mozark Press and the Missouri Humanities Council.

Cover photo: Used by permission, John Hacker

Contents

FOREWORD

Even for those of us who live in the area of the United States known as "Storm Country" or "Tornado Alley," the results of the May 22, 2011, tornado which struck Joplin, Missouri, were stunningly catastrophic. Fortunately, a phone call to Joplin Writers' Guild Chapter President Claudia Mundell the next day revealed her members were reasonably safe and had not suffered major losses. As Claudia reported the spotty news she was able to put together without benefit of cell phone or Internet access, we began to discuss what efforts we might be able to provide to reach out to the community.

The following day, Claudia suggested an anthology dealing with the topic of weather. "One thing about it," she said, "we have it all here, and in varying degrees." The cornerstone for the anthology was set.

By this time, I had been able to reach the Joplin Public Library, which, since it was out of the direct line of the tornado, became the heart of the devastated community and a central communication center. Through the public library, I learned about the losses at the school district and was given the school administration's contact number. A few calls later, it became apparent that the school district had suffered tremendous losses, including libraries, books and other educational resources.

The call for submissions for *Storm Country: The Anthology* opened the next day as a part of the Joplin Book Drive efforts of the Missouri Writers' Guild. This community service project attracted 337 submissions, all from individuals who indicated they just wanted to lend a hand and be a part of Joplin's healing. As Claudia put it, "Not everybody can carry steel and lift walls and not everybody can cook, so everybody does what they can, and writers write."

I am proud to be a part of the community of creative individuals whose work is represented on these pages, but I am especially proud of the spirit in which this work is shared.

Deborah Marshall
President
Missouri Writers' Guild

PREFACE

When Deb Marshall asked if I would like to help with the production of *Storm Country*, I was honored. I had firsthand knowledge of how much she and other area writers and educators had contributed to the relief effort for Joplin schools, and I was anxious to read submissions to the anthology. The eclectic collection of voices in this volume speaks to the many ways in which people respond to crisis and catastrophe: with defiance, resilience, acceptance, and strength. With *Storm Country*, Midwesterners, their families, and friends have once again come together in support of each other during a difficult time. The stories, poems, and reflections included here are a beautiful and gentle reminder that the strength of one is multiplied many times by the strength of a community.

Dianna Graveman, Guest Editor

ACKNOWLEDGEMENTS

Storm Country: The Anthology would not be possible without the generous contributions of the many people who participated in this project. Our deep appreciation goes to the following people who have made the anthology and the Joplin Book Drive a meaningful community effort to benefit the libraries in the Joplin School District:

Claudia Mundell, for planting the seed of an idea that grew into an anthology, and for being the Joplin Writers' Guild coordinator and editor;

John Hacker, for lending us the striking cover photo;

Elaine Viets, for spreading the word online and helping our many requests "go viral;"

Kelli Allen, Susan Croce Kirkpatrick, Linda Fisher, and Dianna Graveman, for being a great editorial team;

Debbie Heim, Joplin High School Head Librarian, for being a superb contact during a very trying time;

Geoff Giglierano and the Missouri Humanities Council, for providing funding for printing and also promoting *Storm Country* and the Joplin Book Drive;

Harold Ream and Mozark Press, for providing countless hours of publishing expertise, support and friendship; and

the writers and poets who contributed their work to this project.

Blackbirds

—remembering Jim Reed

Here they come, a hundred strong,
marching down the fairway
in a black phalanx,
like Caesar's men back in the days
when a thumb could take a life.
These hunters are adept, combing
the grounds for bugs and buds pummeled
by the storm last night.

Everything's in disarray.

Hailstones shattered the earth
as if to protest the old man's death.
They fell the night his son died, too, fell
like furious tears to earth,
freezing the old man in gloom.

It should have been me, he kept saying, *me*.

His wife of sixty-eight years hears
the hailstones knocking at the pane,
opens her window,
welcomes them into her room.

Gloria Vando

STORM WORDS

SHAUN JORDAN

The lights flicker then die. The sudden loss of white electrical noise offers a serene peace, which is quickly replaced by the sound of rain coming, a wall of it pushing across the fields. I see it rolling our way like a heavy gray fog.

"It's alive," I tell my grandmother. She's sitting by the window, her mind somewhere else. Her face is wrinkled and hollow. Life hasn't made her stronger—it's cracked her open and emptied the stuff right out of her.

She waves me down with a vein-knotted hand. "Hush, Robert. Stop filling the boy's head with your gibberish."

I open my mouth to tell her my name is Nick, but I can't recall if doing so has ever done any good. I let it go and instead I deepen my voice to sound like my grandfather did all those years ago.

"Myrna," I say, "I know it's a bad idea, but I can't shake it. It's something I gotta believe."

Gramma shakes her head, but it's not a voluntary action. She's always saying no.

"Robert," her voice trembles, "Robert."

She pauses. Thunder makes cracks between her words, splits them apart like pieces of rubble. The wind is angry and bullying the house with mocking shoves. I'm listening for the sound of quiet.

"Robert," Gramma says, "I ought to have you committed."

She's right. She should have put grandfather in a white room and maybe the same goes for me.

The rain arrives. Big drops sound bigger on the tin roof. It's hard to see outside. The little saplings in the front yard bow to the wind; the leaves are punching bags for rain-shaped fists. I could drink the air it's so wet. Gramma wouldn't notice if I left right now.

"What?" I ask Gramma. She's mumbling something I can't hear over the rain.

I move closer to her. We're both just a couple of shadows. Light won't stick to us.

"What?" I ask again, staring out at the gray.

"Robert, you're a fool," Gramma says. "Robert, don't go out there."

My grandfather's name is the one thing she can remember without effort. The rest of our names slipped from her mind like they were greased, and she doesn't try to grasp them anymore. Her voice is small and scared. I *almost* feel guilty, but I'm not the person she's looking for. And anyway, her words couldn't stop him, so they can't stop me.

I think a shifting mass of shadow looks like my grandfather. It's as tall and thin as I am, but I still look up at it. I rub my eyes. I feel like a tired little boy. The rain is the static of a thousand memories all speaking at once. Just beneath the surface of that gray noise I pick out a lone voice—it's a very faint something that bubbles up from just beneath the ocean of memory. I'm floating on The Sea of Twenty Years Ago. I'm eight and very small in this vast place. My grandfather stands over me while I'm curled up on the couch, my cushioned little boat where I ride out the storms.

He says, "Do you know what a storm is?"

I shake my little head. I do know. It is rain, thunder, lightning, and fear. But I say no because I hope he'll tell me different. I hope I can be wrong, especially about the fear, though I can't imagine not being afraid. I can't imagine being as calm as he is.

"It's a living thing," he says. Across the room I hear Gramma clicking her tongue. She does not approve. He turns to her. "Myrna, I know it's a bad idea, but I can't shake it. It's something I gotta believe."

She purses her lips as she rocks in her chair. "Hush, Robert. Stop filling the boy's head with your gibberish."

He turns back to me, ignoring her. "Not all of them are alive, just some. Like the one that's coming now. Some of them, Nicky, are just dead things still dying. There's a few though, once in a while, that are really, really alive. They think about things and do things on purpose. Why? Well, I couldn't say. No one can. I've never met anyone who could understand what a storm is saying."

This last part he looks sad about.

"Robert, I ought to have you committed," Gramma says, not that she means it.

"Maybe so," Grandad says under his breath.

He looks away from me to the window which is propped open by a broken broom handle. The wind coming through the screen is cool and smells good. I don't want to be so afraid. As I crane my neck up to see for myself, a boom of thunder forces me back down. The old windows rattle. The house feels too small when compared to the sky.

The wind is coming from a yawning mouth. Wide open, a cavern of sound.

"This is one is alive," Grandad says. "It's talking."

He turns his head to the left, pointing his right ear toward the window, listening. *What is it saying?* I wonder. I try to listen, too. If there is anything to be heard besides wind and rain and thunder, I cannot hear it. Grandad is determined. He sits for a long time, listening, and except for the storm, no one speaks.

Then he's jumping up and down with excitement.

"I heard it, I heard it!" He shouts. The entire house fills with his joyous shouts. "Heard it, heard it, heard it. Oh, never thought I'd see the day. Not in a million years. Can you hear it?" His eyes have become tiny galaxies brimming with life.

He tousles my hair. I look to Gramma. Concern and worry shine on her face like black sunlight. There's grief and panic in her eyes. I'm too young to know what that looks like, but I know anyway. And if I didn't, I would soon.

Grandad unlatches the door, a tarnished metal hook in a tarnished metal eyelet.

"Robert, you're a fool," Gramma says. This isn't what she meant to say, but she can't take the words back, so she tries to replace them. "Robert, don't go out there."

He doesn't go out. He turns and blows her a kiss. The gesture is soft, but not apologetic. He doesn't say he's sorry for talking crazy, he doesn't try to explain his reasons why, he doesn't offer promises or say sorry for breaking those he already made. He just plants a kiss in the air, and it floats over to her like a white cloud seen in a clean puddle: a tiny perfect thing you can cup in your hands even though you can't touch it.

"I'm just going to talk," he says, and out the door he goes.

Thunder or not, I have to look. I peek over the windowsill and see him run out into the yard. Instantly he's soaked. And then he's washing out, disappearing into the rain. From somewhere far away, I hear Gramma scream, tears sewn into the fabric of her shouts. Maybe she tells him to come back, maybe she curses him for leaving her. I never know because I never hear.

Across the distance I see it form: a black finger pointing down out of the clouds, but spinning like a screw driving into the earth. There is dust and dirt and splinters of things unable to resist the upward denial of gravity. I have no time to make sense of it. I'm snatched off my boat with all the force of a limb being ripped off a tree. Gramma pulls me up and rushes me to the closet in her room. She shoves me in and stands at the door a moment, thinking. The house groans in agony, and that makes up her mind. She dives in and curls around me.

Gramma digs us out. The house gave up, and it's just splinters and shattered bricks. Gramma puts her voice to the air, but it doesn't carry to wherever Grandad is. Silence is all that answers her. Silence is all that *will* ever answer her.

My memory capsizes, and I'm drifting in the current. Gramma is shaking by the window. The air has turned cold. Not rain anymore, but hail sprinkles the yard. I know this is the same storm that took Grandad. It's come back to tell me where to find him.

I barely strain when I lift her and put her somewhere safe. A white cloud kiss and I know why he left. I can hear the storm talking, but I can't understand it. I need to get closer to make sense of what it's saying to me. This one is alive.

Edge of the Storm

Still in the sunlight,
still in the warmth.
I can see next to me the
heavy blue skies of rain.
The wind begins to churn,
mixing my heat with its cool;
rolling, rolling ever toward me.
In the calm of the moment before
its mood strikes with vengeance,
that's where I'll stand waiting.
The birds quiet and find a safe place,
and I should do the same,
but still I stand to stare at the sky:
A line drawn across it like child's chalk
on gray cement; in between, where
the earth is divided into two ragged parts,
much like my mind, or a country road
that winds thru the land and
splices the fields right open.

Jordan Smith

Stormwolves

Day- The spring flowers
have perished to the
conquering tiger lilies,
and the shrieks of
cicadas swell, then die,
under the hot July
copperhead sun.

Dusk- Gray-shapes
made of dark clouds
and electric wind
stalk the dying day,
claw red lines across
the belly of the sky.

Night- The stormwolves
prowl, then leap
from behind the hills.
Lope across the tangled
glass water of the lake.
Howl over the tangled
glass water of the lake.
Charge upon the shore,
crack cedar limbs,
snap and bite a path.
Leave a trail of brown
needles and bloody sap.

Todd Hanks

A Piccadilly Circus Elephant Helps Clear Debris

Past the Erbie Cemetery where Thurman Martin's kin
Have lain for generations, we clear brush
In the distant roar of the firestorm, sky dark with smoke.
Like roman candles, a row of cedars bursts into flame
And the natives start their ragged dance.
See a spark. Stomp the grass. Hop-skip over snakes.
We dance the fire out and pass a jug of water. An ordinary
thing.
Our homes are saved. The pie supper's on for Tuesday.
Crazy Harold Camping said the world would end May 21.
It didn't. It ended the next day for Joplin neighbors
In a deafening roar at 5:34. Homes burst into splinters.
Sky black with dust. No time now for stomping.
Cancel the circus. Pass the jug of water.
Pie suppers will start soon.

Kathryn Buckstaff

January 23, 1958

He tells the same story
as though oblivious
to how patience, like frost,
changes depending on where
in the month we have landed.
His voice explains a wet cover
inert and stubborn, insistence
claiming grass with thin leftover
webs spindled through blades—
the ice a magic assurance
before this late winter hunt.

He explains each detail
with practiced detachment, closed
to the secrets contained
in the way the buck's hair
will lay matted in likely swirls,
tunnels for beetles and worse
to take what they can. Before

we have come to the part
in his tale where violently cooling
flesh is sectioned into soft chunks,
he reminds us how the cutting was blind
against such massive busts of white
and cold as this tale's winter, that morning's
storm. Heading long into first morning

with the meat, he says to struggle against
the climb back home, was to admit
acceptance of the freeze. Here, always,

he pauses, hoarding the moment to recount
one more time, the exact shading
shell-pearl gray, of the crystalline frost
making a perfect, delicate dagger
of each lash surrounding the buck's black eye.

Kelli Allen

GOLDEN LILACS UNDER THE WORM MOON

DONNA VOLKENANNT

"It is now nine-twenty," a shrill voice droned over a loudspeaker. "The mall closes in ten minutes."

Lil eased herself into a chair at the food court and planted her shopping bag and purse between her swollen ankles. Her stomach churned; a deep cough rattled her chest. When her breathing calmed, she raked a hand, thin and mottled like a fallen oak leaf, through her silver hair.

"Please head for the nearest exit," the intercom blared.

Shopping bag in hand and purse draped over a shoulder, Lil trundled toward the red signs, wondering where the day had gone. She remembered talking to Tommy on the phone after eating a cup of chicken noodle soup for lunch. Before they hung up, he told her not to take the car out. Sleet and freezing rain were headed her way.

If the State of Missouri judged me fit to drive at age eighty-seven, who is Tommy to tell me I can't?

After washing dishes, she dotted rouge on her pale cheeks, buttoned her white linen jacket, and kissed her parakeet Gracie goodbye. On the way to her car, she inhaled a hint of early spring as she passed postage-stamp gardens of budding tulips and daffodils. Next thing she remembered, she was sitting in the mall restaurant at suppertime. When the waitress brought her a slice of lemon meringue pie, she urged Lil to be careful because a thief had been snatching purses in the mall.

She rubbed her back and shifted her bag. As she shuffled behind knots of noisy teenagers heading for the exits, she clutched her purse to her chest, worried one of them might steal her driver's license or social security card.

Wouldn't that be a pickle?

At each door, she hesitated, trying to remember where she'd parked. Confused, she traipsed back to the food court. When a strong hand touched her shoulder, the hairs on the back of her neck bristled. She closed her eyes and prayed.

"Excuse me, Ma'am," a deep voice said.

Lil turned and stared into the pock-marked face of a young man dressed in a coal-colored uniform. His eyes were close together and dull as dirt.

He tapped the silver badge on his chest. "Time to go. Storm's almost here."

Unable to find her voice, Lil gaped at him, thankful he wasn't the thief.

He leaned closer and shouted. "Need help finding your way?"

"I do not!" She turned from his sour breath. "And no need to shout. I'm old, but I'm not deaf."

Who did he think he was—an impudent pup like him asking if I need help? Before that boy's mother was out of diapers I was milking cows and butchering hogs.

Lil thrust out her chin and left through the nearest door. Cold rain pelted her uncovered head and soaked her thin jacket as she wandered outside, watching headlights crisscross the parking lot and the last bus for the night drive away.

Now isn't that just like March in Missouri—sunshine and daffodils at daybreak, snow and sleet by nightfall.

As the rain turned to ice, she headed for the bus stop. Her feet lost purchase and she slipped on the sidewalk, banging her head and biting her tongue. The coppery taste of blood filled her mouth. She staggered to the bench and huddled in a dark corner, shivering as she tried to remember what her car looked like.

At first she thought she used the Buick—the one Norbert drove to Mass on Sunday and the fish fry at the Legion Hall on Friday nights. But she knew that couldn't be right. After her husband passed away, Tommy sold the farm and the Buick, moved her into an apartment, and bought her a new car. The new one was smaller, and it wasn't blue—Norbert's favorite color.

Norbert. His name brought an ache to her heart and a catch in her throat. She missed him so. The first time he told her he loved her was after he came home from fighting in Germany, wearing his Army uniform with rows full of ribbons and shiny brass buttons.

Seems like yesterday.

He'd stopped by the farmhouse, carrying a bouquet of lilacs and a wicker basket. Lil removed a patchwork quilt from the clothesline, and in the soft grass beneath an oak tree they picnicked on his mother's fried chicken, homemade bread, and fresh strawberry jam. In a hushed voice, he told her about his shell shock after fighting Nazis. Then he got down on one knee and asked her to marry him. Bought his first Buick for their honeymoon.

Now, what was that car Tommy traded the Buick for? She remembered it was named after a planet.

Was it Mars? No. Mars was Norbert's favorite candy before he got diabetes. After that, he ate tapioca pudding or bananas for dessert.

Venus? Whenever that song came on, he twirled her around the kitchen and called her his "Goddess of Love."

Land's sake Norbert was so fun loving, yet full of regret after Mary Grace.

"Saturn," she yelled and laughed out loud. She remembered her car had the same name as the god of agriculture. She must've walked past her white car a dozen times. Now it sat on the parking lot, looking like an igloo all covered with ice. Her knees buckled when she tried to stand. She sat back down and closed her eyes.

Rest will make me strong again, just like after Mary Grace.

She shivered awake. The sleet had stopped. The sky cleared and a full moon cast a shimmering light across the glazed parking lot.

"The Worm Moon," she said nodding towards heaven.

In fourth grade she'd been the only student who knew the full moon in March is called the Worm Moon. Sister Maria Isidore gave her a gold star. Lil learned about the moons in *The Old Farmer's Almanac*. She also read how the earth softens at the beginning of spring and worms crawl to the surface. If the sun gets hot, the worms get burned. In a hard frost they freeze, unable to crawl back into the warm ground.

She picked at her icy collar and squinted at a man in uniform gliding her way. At first, she thought it was the guard with the sour breath—until the smell of lilacs filled the air.

"Norbert?"

She shook her head, thinking it was a dream. She closed her eyes, trying to remember what she had to tell him. Something about Mary Grace and the Nazis.

The morning after their wedding, Norbert reminded her about his shell shock when she touched his arm and he squeezed her hand so hard she cried. He apologized so many times she lost count.

Since then she knew never to wake him suddenly. But the night her water broke, hard labor started right away—nothing like when Tommy was born. When she shook Norbert's shoulder, he knocked her off the bed. He was on top of her with fists raised—a wild look in his eyes. By the time he woke from his nightmare and carried her back to bed, blood ran down her legs all over their quilt.

Later, Doc Brinker delivered Mary Grace. He bundled her in a pink blanket and laid her on Lil's chest. In a soft voice, he told them Mary Grace was a blue baby. Her cord got wrapped around her neck and cut off her oxygen. Said he doubted the baby would make it till morning. And because of all the bleeding, Lil wouldn't be able to have more children.

"Good thing we've got Tommy," Norbert had said.

Like her precious baby girl didn't matter.

After Mary Grace died, Norbert treated her like "Queen for a Day." He bought her expensive presents—even a hi-fi and a color TV—but all the gifts in the world couldn't make up for losing Mary Grace. Over the years, Lil's heart grew as cold and empty as her womb.

On Norbert's deathbed, she told him what a good husband and provider he'd been. She knew there were three more words he wanted to hear, but those words stuck in her throat.

A brisk wind caught her breath. She peeled open her eyes. Her hands shook and a chill ran down her spine. In front of her Norbert stood, handsome as the day he got down on his knee.

In one hand he held out a bouquet of lilacs that glimmered golden in the moonlight. In his other arm he cradled a pink blanket that wiggled with tiny fists and feet poking out from underneath.

"Mary Grace?"

Lil's heart felt light as a snowflake. She took a soft breath and remembered those three words she needed to say.

"I forgive you," she whispered and reached out for the golden lilacs.

An earlier version of this short story appeared in the 2004 *Mid Rivers Review Literary Journal*.

Hard Rain

An old song of yours kept playing in my head
while I watched freezing rain coat the world.
I could hear you singing in that voice of yours
while trees bowed to the hard rain
and dropped from exhaustion.
My river birch outlasted the pear trees next door,
but finally crashed and shattered,
taking bits of the house with it.

Four days later, we're out on the patio with
a rake, pruning shears, busted chain saw, and a toolbox.
What would you do if you were here, Bob Dylan?
Strum your guitar and sing a few verses about
the workingman up in the cherry picker
trying to get the power on?
Write something eloquent about the trees
with their spiky broken tops pointing up to Heaven?
Sing a ballad for the birds, so rudely evicted during a storm?
Maybe you'd know how to fix a chain saw.
Maybe you'd help us clean up this mess.

Cheryl Davis

Hope in a Barrel

Michelle O'Brien

It was May 28, 2011—five days after an F-5 tornado struck and decimated the town of Joplin, Missouri. We had made a very quick decision to drive down and lend a hand to the reeling city.

My dear friend Tammy and I had spent much time trying to find the best place to report for cleanup duty. We contacted the Joplin City Manager's office and were given an option to join in with the Search and Rescue teams, but since we were two families with five children, placing them in a situation where they might come face-to-face with death—human or animal—was simply not an option.

We arrived at 10:30 a.m., a little off our intended timeframe, ready to work.

"Children under eighteen can't assist in the debris fields," a heavy-set redhead quipped impatiently from behind the makeshift volunteer counter.

"No worries," I said brightly. "Someone somewhere can use our help."

Ahead of us in line were two ladies, each with a dog on a leash. The looks of dismay on Sonnie, Cheyenne, Wellesley, Savannah, and Garret's faces quickly disappeared amidst the licks and wags being doled out by the warm, wriggling canines.

The dogs were Pet Therapy animals, and their companions, Carol and Freda, had come to the University to see what they and their furry friends could do to help. Both ladies were nurses at St. John's Hospital, a nine story building that had been wiped out after suffering a direct hit. Incredibly, Freda's home, place of employment and neighborhood *were* in the seven miles of ruin, yet here she was looking to lend aid to others.

Tammy and I quickly traded glances and knew immediately what we needed to do.

"Freda, can we come and help you at your house?"

She stared at us stunned before replying incredulously, "Would you?"

We exchanged cell phone numbers and agreed to meet up with her at her home after a planned stop at the YMCA.

Joplin's YMCA South was taking donations of all sorts, but more importantly, they were working hard to entertain the children of the area—some who had lost their homes, some who had lost their loved ones and many who had lost both.

Our five youngsters moved into the roles of mentors and guides instantaneously. A little boy attached himself to my daughter Sonnie's leg the moment we walked through the gym doors. I too had an impish hitchhiker adhered to my thigh. Destiny was her name.

"Can I help you pass out cookies?" the adorable brunette second grader said to me. We weren't "allowed" to have the Joplin kiddos helping us, but here this gorgeous girl had lost her home, and *I* was supposed to tell her she couldn't give out treats? Not in this lifetime!

I came home with a stuffed pig, aptly named Knuckles, personally autographed by my favorite Joplin seven-year-old. It's a curly-tailed treasure that is forever priceless to me. Written in bold black Sharpie marker on its pink back are these words:

Destiny

Love U

We jumped in our trucks, keyed in the address and followed the GPS to Freda's house. Military personnel were stationed at various intersections directing traffic. There were no working stoplights in this part of Joplin and no stop signs. I remember thinking how surreal to hear the landmarks Freda gave us.

"There's a white pickup in the driveway, a red one that's wrecked with all the windows blown out and it's sideways against the house. Oh, and next door to us there's a van flipped upside down in the yard."

We found parking adjacent to a house that looked as if an enormous hand had reached down and ripped away the entire front wall. How eerie it felt to be gazing into someone's house at a child's bed, a TV sitting unscathed on a stand and a couch with a side table, neat as a pin, right next to it. No roof, no wall, no windows—a cutaway view of someone's former life.

Grabbing gloves and bottled water, we walked to Freda's. The house immediately across the street, belonging to an elderly woman, was absolutely flattened except for a back bedroom. The woman had lived in that room for three days, too afraid to come out.

Birds had nowhere to land and took up residence in damaged houses, flying neatly in and out of holes left by debris that had punched through walls and windows. Trees had been uprooted and power lines were down, swept along by gale force winds and fired, like rockets, into peoples' homes.

The fragments of debris were all about the size of your palm or smaller. Sure, there were larger remains—recognizable pieces of roof, siding, walls, drywall—but for the most part, the wreckage was if everything had been put through an industrial wood chipper and sprayed all over the city.

"It's like eating noodles," Tammy said, suddenly at my side. "You keep taking bites, but every time you look down, the bowl seems just as full."

"You're right," I agreed sadly. "That's exactly how it feels."

We were gladly interrupted by one of the girls squealing excitedly, "Look what I found!" Opening a muddy glove, she revealed an iridescent porcelain angel, wings outstretched and completely intact.

We had been finding personal items all day and were gently separating them from the rest of the debris. All the kids had found many, many items. Each one a treasure, shared and exclaimed over before being reverently placed in the growing pile.

Our children were amazing. They carried debris and dragged fence posts still encased in concrete across lawns. They raked, bagged, and paired up to carry the "extra" heavy stuff. We watched them encourage one another, do us proud with their manners and make new friends with their willingness to help wherever, whenever and with whatever. Ultimately, they wound up at a house that looked like a giant had ripped the front wall open. The owner, sifting through the fragments himself, said if the kids would help him go through the things in the garage, they could keep anything they could find. A treasure hunt amidst tragedy—little did we know our greatest gem was yet to come!

"Dog!" Cheyenne yelped excitedly. She ducked down and peered again into the blue plastic barrel we uncovered beneath a ruined section of shed wall. The drum was laid over on its side and did not move easily.

"There's a dog in the barrel," she announced matter-of-factly after a second look.

"Alive?" I asked.

She grinned and nodded gleefully.

Tammy and I dropped to our knees and peered in the drum. Sure enough, gazing back at us from the gloomy depths of the blue barrel was a tiny dog walled in by mud, leaves and sticks.

"Way to go, Cheyenne!" we cheered.

Looking in on our lovely little survivor again, I was worried. The dog hadn't moved. Five days is a long time to go without water. Fortunately, the shed wall section had shielded it from the sun for many days.

Right now, however, out from under that protective covering, the barrel was sweltering.

I began digging the debris out, cooing softly to the dog as I went, moving ever nearer.

"Be careful, Mom," I heard Sonnie say, her voice colored with concern and growing anticipation.

Cheyenne and Tammy were crouched down behind me while the rest of the kiddos knelt in a ring expectantly. A crowd had gathered; a little bud of hope was blooming in this razed neighborhood.

The dog seemed to know we were trying to help. Wide, soft brown eyes, so wary yet so trusting, watched me from the back of the hot drum. Finally, I was able to reach in and gently stroke—her!

"Are you sure it's a female?" Freda asked from beside me.

"Yup," I confirmed from inside the hot drum. "Definitely no stem on this apple."

"I'm going to just grab her," I announced finally.

"Get her by the nape," Freda, who coincidentally raises and shows dogs, instructed.

Doing just that, I pulled out our beautiful brown and black barrel dog. She was petite with floppy bat-like ears, one of the most gorgeous things I'd ever seen! Freda gathered her up and carried her to the waiting SUV, looking like the Pied Piper as she crossed to her vehicle—our five children strung out behind her like dusty pearls.

My Foundation

What happened to the life we built together?
Where did it go? The twisted tree trunks point the way.
Was I so bad that all we had was taken from us?
Did the beginning of the end begin today?

I wonder who will find your state fair ribbons.
Or our vacation money in the Mason jar.
Will they find the pieces of your grandma's tea set?
Are we covered for the house that crushed our car?

Everything we worked and scratched and saved for
Took a heartbeat and a thunderstorm to lose.
Those little bands that play on Beale Street know their music,
But if they're not here, they'll never know the blues.

Where will we go to get out of the weather?
Are we supposed to crawl back under the debris?
The only things that we have left are what we're wearing.
Our life will never be the way it used to be.

Then you tell me life is more than state fair ribbons.
And you fold your muddy fingers over mine.
And like the barn dance when you led me to the dance floor,
You smile and whisper, "We'll take one step at a time."

Bill Cairns

It Rained

Cully Bryant

It rained and rained and the Mississippi swelled like a bloated possum dead on the side of a southeast Missouri highway. The levee creaked and strained, and maybe it would have held. Maybe it wouldn't have. Maybe Cairo and Carbondale and Timbuktu would have been flooded like the days of Noah. We'll never know.

But when the slurry was touched off and all hell broke loose, a TV reporter standing miles away from the blast jumped at the sound like she'd been shot—and as sand that had been hauled by mules and men eighty years ago flew through the night sky, the Mississippi stopped swelling. It stopped swelling and started roaring and crashing through the spillway like blood exploding from a ruptured artery.

As it caromed about the land, driving deer and turkey to high ground, if they were lucky enough to find any, it burst upon its old haunts from long ago. Like stagnant molasses, it oozed where it was unwanted. Houses abandoned recently unwillingly became aquariums filled with turtles and snakes and slime. Down the road a church was transformed into a dirty swimming pool without swimmers or a lifeguard, its pews bouncing around inside like neglected rafts. Behind that church was a graveyard—a small one out back. I wonder about it now. Were the souls resting there disturbed? Did they think the trumpet had sounded, that final trumpet marking today as *The Day*? Did they rise up from their earthen beds expecting to see Gabriel and the bright, bright light of day after so many years in the darkness, only to find black water? I wonder if they floated away never to be found again, their gray bones rattling and clattering in the tumult, or if they latched onto a casket handle with a withered hand and held on, straining against the current.

I saw pictures taken by men in boats of sights bizarre to behold. Peacocks on rooftops cried for their master. Purple martens flying low over the brand new ocean looked like waterfowl, their homes once so lofty now skimming the water's surface like aluminum lily pads. The scene suggested an agrarian Venice with bearded, suspendered farmers-turned-gondoliers patrolling the waterways on the lookout for a familiar landmark.

And then it stopped raining. After its holiday on the farm, the river unwillingly trudged back to where it belonged, leaving behind dead catfish and carp on the roads, water-logged pews, wet peacocks, confused martens, mud and stink. Now that it's gone, they can go back—all of them—the gondoliers-turned-back-to-farmers and the rest. They will wring out their homes the best they can and plant beans—those who are able.

But that hole is still there—the one they exploded—and if you squint and shade your eyes you can see it on the horizon. Its presence leaves them feeling exposed and vulnerable. Who knows what may tumble through next? They have heard it will be repaired, but even the best wrought plans can come undone.

Someday it will rain again.

A Different Way to Pray

I know what it feels like to stand where
my house once was, and not know where I am

wrapped in disbelief, knee deep
in the aftermath of our neighborhood

I remember what it feels like to be
momentarily unable to breathe

> *That there will be something soft for under
> your feet, to pillow them after you've walked
> through the glass.*

There is so little left to the imagination
when the unimaginable becomes everyday

when the elders volunteer to sacrifice their stories
wearing themselves out instead, putting out our fires

and children who no longer speak their own pain
wander through the scorched remains of ours

> *That there will be cool hands to soothe and draw
> the burning from your forehead when the fire
> boils your skin*

The memory of terror and the fear of it
recurring shatter our plans for recovery

true happiness becomes a resolution to
give up all hope of anything but bittersweet

and life turns into getting by without breaking
down, even if our lives depend on it

That there will be a face that's familiar,
an honest smile, and tenderness to
open your heart.

Rosalie O'Leary

Tornado Bear

was a consolation prize. I am positive that he had a tail when I packed him away. Now, there's a hole, an unexpected window. Mice, moths? Maybe. But it seems like sudden destruction.

What I remember: It was inventory time at the stainless steel factory. Mom had to work late, counting. I had Pink Dress Barbie, with matching shoes and boa. I was being good for the Nice Lady at the reception desk. Barbie had removed her matching shoes and boa to play in the sand/ beige Berber carpet.

The Nice Lady has decayed into less than bones in my memory: a disembodied voice answers the phone dutifully by the third ring. She sounds afraid, and I look up from my beach. At 5 I thought it might have been God. And though it sounds false to say that events happened so fast there was hardly a pause, a line from a made for TV movie, probably a crime drama, possibly featuring Tom Selleck, nevertheless, it happened so fast there was hardly a pause.

"What? Where? How long?" She sounds afraid and I look up from my beach at the fear-twisted face of the Nice Lady and the glass doors swing open closed open closed it's like magic but not the good Disney kind and she screams "Come here NOW" and I run with Barbie, without question, and the lights go out and I hit the reception desk and I cry for my mom and the Nice Lady picks me up and we run to a dark room full of people and she yells "Gwen? Gwen? Gwen!" and it should be loud I'm sure it's loud but it's quiet too, the sound is pulled from my ears like a magician pulls a scarf in a trick and I see sky but there wasn't a window and then my mom's there and she is holding me and we cry.

It had to be a monster. Wind cools my face through the car window on the highway, brushing my hair back, like the girls on TV. A scary monster had poked its long destructive finger down on us like you would poke at a large bug. Poke, squeal, withdraw. Repeat after suitable interval. Never mind the now broken wing. Safety was just another thing for babies, filed between ruffles and training pants. Now tornadoes were inevitable, like cereal at breakfast and cold chills during the opening theme of Unsolved Mysteries. My poor Barbie forever after suffered cold chills bought on by bare shoulders and feet. Somewhere a bird's eggs hatched into hot pink feathery fluff; an old bachelor, drinking a cheap beer, scratched his belly in the yard, and stared at an inexplicable tiny shoe nestled in the grass.

The bear appeared the next day—a post-Christmas sales rack special. He was Tornado Bear, my consolation prize; a talisman to ward off the monster, every time the sirens blared.

Shiloh Peters

Thunderboomer

April batters Ozark afternoon.
Redbuds bleed purple
on the lawn. Gray munches
all the way down
to toe-stumbling roots
tickling squirrels into speed.
The house cries dark
with hope. You rise
from the breakfast wasteland
we savored like hipbones.
I follow you into the bedroom
where you curl
against me, the wind
smacking then cupping
the front door into peace,
into giving up.
You are melty as butter.
Clouds blacken outside
like toast. Our fingers
hum like thunder.

Dave Malone

Ruminating

The day the barn blew down,
silence claimed the cow's attention.
When birds and crickets stilled,
she looked up from the sweet green grass.

Thus it was she witnessed
the shuddering twist of the barn
collapsing on itself
and a winter's worth of hay.

Now, a full year later,
she sometimes stops her grazing
and lifts her head
to eye the sky.

Teddi Doleski

It's Raining Snakes!

Bev Rohlf

As I stepped on the grass in our front yard, my feet depressed as if stepping on a sponge. It had rained steadily and sometimes heavily for over a week. The soil couldn't absorb any more. The earthworms were seeking relief by crawling onto any solid surface, concrete, the driveway, downstairs patio, the asphalt in front of our home.

It was an unusual spring; unusual for the heavy rain and for the sighting of so many snakes around our home. Before the rain, my husband had seen garden snakes numbering seven or so sunning themselves in a small flower garden by the front door. They wiggled so much, the ground appeared to be moving. Another snake was dead in the cul-de-sac, curled in front of our home. My granddaughter picked up a five-inch ring snake and thrust it in my face for approval. Later we saw a medium-sized snake in the garage a few feet from the kitchen door, and I swept it out to the road with a broom.

My daughter told me—from her experience in a sweat lodge in Colorado—that some American Indians believe a snake entering one's home means that something will change in the lives of the people who live there. I wondered what might happen.

By May, the heavy rain had moved us indoors and snakes were no longer the topic of conversation. Then a strange thing happened. Early one Sunday morning during a severe rainstorm, I sat up in bed as though shot from a cannon. My mind screamed at me over and over to get to the basement, go to the basement.

I ran out of the bedroom, across the dining room, and down the stairs to the walkout basement family room. Looking around, I saw a dark line like a long pencil close to the stairs and a few feet east of the patio doors. Farther away, I saw a small, black object like an earthworm. I worked through my adrenaline to shake off the deep sleep so that I could recognize what I was seeing. Yes, you got it. It was a small ring snake that had escaped the rain by crawling under the patio doors. It was able to get in because the screen door had been left back to the side, leaving an opening.

I grabbed some tissue and picked up the tiny snake and threw it outside, back into the rain. God help it. Now, I wondered, with my heart pounding, could the straight dark object be something besides a long pencil or stick the kids might have brought in. Again, I tried to focus my eyes sharply. Fortunately, there was a small sheet of cardboard on the card table, the torn back of a notebook. I leaned down and pushed with the cardboard at the far end of the dark line. It began to wiggle, writhing and twisting, and turning. I struggled to keep my composure and pushed it toward the door. As soon as it was off the carpet and on the concrete, it raced to the rock garden like a speeding arrow.

I don't know if the Indian legend is true, but a few weeks later my mother was diagnosed with cancer. I do know that when it rains, I hurry to check the screen door.

Prairie Wolf Wind

The prairie wolf wind howls outside my door.
He thrums signboards and snaps off the branches of trees.
He pries at roof tiles and knocks over trash cans.
He huffs and he puffs and says he'll blow my house down.
It isn't built of straw,
Nor made from sticks and twigs.
But I hope he doesn't start circling round and around.
Cause this old trailer home might take a notion to fly,
It has no wings or landing gear.
It would be much the worse for its flight,
When it comes on back down.

DeAnna Quietwater Noriega

AN AUGUST AFTERNOON

JOHN CUNNINGHAM

The phone rang inside but neither of them got up to answer it. The house was too hot to be gabbing. Bill and Mildred sat in their old wooden rocking chairs, husband and wife passing away the quiet country afternoon in the shade of their covered porch. Mildred had a magazine open on her lap, reading, while Bill kept glancing up at the thermometer nailed to a post beside him, waiting for the little dial to close the gap between lines and finally read one hundred degrees.

"Hot as a son of a gun out," Bill said, wiping his face with a kerchief that he replaced in his pocket.

Mildred looked at him over her glasses. "I bet they have air condition at your doctor's office. Maybe we ought to go there."

"Oh, would you just cut that crap out?"

"Why are you being so stubborn?"

"Mildred, I wish you'd drop it."

"I still don't understand why you won't go."

"There's nothing to see," Bill said, picking at a splinter in his chair. He looked up at the hazy, blue-white sky. Not a cloud in sight. "Sure do wish it'd rain."

Mildred didn't respond, fanning herself instead with her magazine as she rocked slowly, her eyes fixed on the white rocks of the long drive and the short stalks of yellow grass, bleached by the heat and sun. The scorched lawn spread out in every direction, shimmering as it neared the road that marked the edge of their property. A single grove of trees stood to the left of the drive, their leaves and branches sagging from lack of rain.

"Lawn ain't got a shot in this heat," Bill went on, "not without the rain. Glad I didn't plant any crops this year."

"They'd have made it."

"Bah!" Bill said, stifling a cough. "Not like they used to. We used to grow bushels and bushels. Like to see you do that in this." He waved his hand toward the base of the steps, as if the heat were a man waiting for Bill to invite him up onto the porch.

"You were a lot younger then."

"We sure were," Bill said, smiling suddenly. "You remember the first time we took Sarah out into the cornfields?"

Mildred laughed. "And the scarecrow scared her instead of the crows?"

"What'd we chase her for? Ten minutes?"

"Oh, at least fifteen. Through the corn. She wouldn't eat it that entire winter."

They fell silent as the reverie took a seat between them, much as their daughter had done on lazy days when they had all been much younger. Bill coughed again, a raspy thing that turned his face red. It lasted a few seconds, and when he finished, he cussed and cleared his throat. "You know, Jeb Nelson died in heat like this."

Mildred sighed.

"Well, he did. Remember? They found him a week later, rotting away in his own living room."

"He didn't have any children."

"What's that got to do with the price of eggs?"

"If he'd have had kids, they could have taken care of him."

Bill laughed bitterly. "I wouldn't count on it."

"Good Lord, Bill, she just got a new job. You can't expect her to drop everything and rush here."

"Well, if she didn't live on the other side of the world."

"She lives in Austin, Bill."

"Like I said, the other side of the world."

"It's a couple hours' plane ride. She said she'd be here Friday. Can't you wait two days?"

Bill grumbled and pulled his pipe from his breast pocket, chewing on the stem. They could take the tobacco away from him, but God damn them straight to hell if they tried to take the pipe away, too. A car rushed past out on the road, gone almost as soon as it came. The slightest whisper of a breeze reached them on the porch.

"It was the heat that got him," Bill said.

"Say again?"

"That got Jeb. They said on the news that his cancer finally got him, but it was the heat."

"I'm sure the cancer had a little something to do with it."

Bill huffed dismissively. "People can live *years* with cancer. The heat'll get ya every time if you're not careful."

Mildred stopped fanning herself and looked over at Bill.

"Don't look at me like that, woman," Bill said.

"Bill—"

"Go make yourself useful and pour me a glass of tea, would ya?"

Sighing, Mildred put down her magazine and went inside to get the tea. Another car drove by out on the road, this one slow enough for Bill to make out the driver. A man drove with his arm sticking out the window. He turned and looked over for a second, the disinterested gaze of a man seeing something other than flat grassland and the gray ribbon of the road and unable to help but look. Bill could just make out the golden locks of the passenger before the car rounded the corner and was gone.

The screen door opened with a whine and Mildred came back out onto the porch, handing Bill his tea. He thanked her with a grunt. The sun had been creeping up onto the porch all afternoon, and now it had finally chased away the shade, swallowing Mildred's chair along with the entire right side of the porch. Scooting the rocker closer to Bill, she sat for a second before picking up her magazine and fanning herself.

"Maybe you should drink green tea. I heard it's good for you."

"I doubt it'd do much good," Bill said.

"You never know."

The next car that drove by they recognized as the neighbor's. The green Chevy slowed and a hand waved to them before it, too, rounded the bend. Bill waved back even though the car was gone.

"There went Brian. I wonder if he's coming back from the lake."

"On a Wednesday?"

"Well, it is summertime. Maybe he's on vacation."

Mildred brushed at the tiny whine and itch of a gnat in her ear. "I didn't think carpenters got vacations if they weren't in the union."

"Everybody gets a vacation."

"Well, I could sure use one. My hip hurts from all this humidity."

Bill looked over at her and chuckled. "Are you kidding? This is it, honey. You're on vacation. The Golden Years aren't so golden, are they?"

Bill coughed again, his third spell the worst yet.

"That sounds like it's getting worse. You know, I bet there's *something* they can still do," Mildred said. "They couldn't have tried everything."

"They tried everything," Bill grumbled.

"Maybe if we went somewhere else."

"Every place is the same."

"I heard about a place up in Chicago. Maybe we could look it up."

"They got great catfishing at that lake Brian goes to. I ever tell you that?"

"A hundred times. How about it? Want to give them a call?"

"Brian told me he caught a twelve pounder there. A twelve pounder! I've never even seen one that big."

"The hell with the lake, Bill. This is serious."

"Damn it all, Mildred! Don't disturb a man when he's dreaming of catfish!"

Mildred sat stunned for a moment before sniffing and opening her magazine.

"I think I'm gonna drive into town tomorrow," Bill said when the silence had dragged on for several minutes. "I ought to make sure things are in order."

Neither spoke for a long time, both sitting and listening to the shrill call of the birds and the low hum of insects.

"Shut up and drink your tea," Mildred said finally, fanning herself once again.

Bill rubbed his stubbled face and looked down at his shoes. They were a sorry sight, the leather scuffed and faded. Right where his toes met his feet they were creased and cracked, with a hole on either shoe on the instep, right where they started to curve to trace the arch of his foot. They had been so sturdy once. The leather had been strong and brown, had had a deep, rich smell. They had been party to years of fruitful harvests and hearty winters, a regular go-to, sure-fire thing.

Bill resumed rocking and looked back out at his lawn, out at the heat that melted the very air above the asphalt of the road.

"I love you, Mildred," he whispered. "I always have."

Mildred turned to him, her eyes heavy with tears. "I know."

40

Heat
(to be read languidly with sweating brow)

Eighty-four degrees
        And
it is not   quite   noon
To be   this hot
a place should have
something   going for it

California has   beaches
        surfboards
                and bikini
                tan lines   so small
                your tongue erases
                        then while searching

Texas has   cowgirls
in snap-button shirts
        tails knotted
        below breasts   coated
        with the
        tangy   essence   or sweat

Arizona has   spring training
        baseball   surrounded by
        Saguaro cactus
        fingers   of hot   shade
        for lazy   Gila monsters
                and
        more   cowgirls

There is nothing here

Not wanting to offend
I won't say   where I am
Only that   all I see is
        humidity
        obesity
        Kansas Cidity
        timidity
                and
probably many more
"idities"   it is too hot
to even   think about

Jerry-Mac Johnston

Greensburg, KS

hadn't seen it coming,
wrapped in hail and rain,
and the cloud-dampened sun
receded to its rest.
Storm sirens blared dread –
a 20-min. warning –
ways of escape cut off.
9:45 P.M. on Friday, it struck –
a mile-and-a-half wide
and wedge-shaped,
gunmetal gray
against black sky, eerie
with chartreuse streaks –
a creature out of legend
from when Kiowa roamed.
The townspeople chose
to sprout anew
like hard white spring wheat
from pounded prairie.
Rebuilt homes revive
the Sun Dance, stand as icons
to mischievous Sendeh,
who they know first hand
still play tricks with wind
over their fields.

Karin Frank

THE AFTERNOON AIR

ANNE GRADY

Her mother was quiet finally. They stood in the yard, halfway between the house and the equipment shed at the back of the yard which sloped down to a cornfield. Her mother stood there, one hand over her mouth, the other hand clutching Meg's hand too tightly, digging her nails into Meg's palm. "That hurts," Meg screamed. "Let me go." Her mother didn't hear, and Meg yelled again. Her mother eased her grip but didn't let go. She said nothing. The whole world was quiet. Not a chirp or buzz or the sound of a motor crossed the afternoon air.

Before, everything had been so loud. Her mother was screaming then, as Meg ran and twirled through the house. The wind howled in the trees and the house joined in the wail. It shuddered and rattled and shuddered and rattled all around them. Everything was very loud and very dark. The colors from the windows were green and black.

Meg ran in circles throughout the first floor while her mother screamed at her to come to her, come to her right now. Her mother chased her and tackled her in the living room. She clasped her arms under Meg's arms and around her chest, and dragged her down the hall to the bathroom. She threw her into the tub and got in on top of her, screaming and crying, her bones pushing right through Meg, pushing her down.

Then they were outside, standing in the yard. The old, empty corn crib across the road and down at the next corner was gone. Meg had heard her mother complain to her father about that abandoned crib and its owner many times. "A disgrace," she called it. The disgrace was gone now. Some of its warped, colorless boards were scattered around the field of small soy bean plants. Most of it was just gone. Some boards from their house were ripped down and gone too.

Then it was Meg's turn to wail. The tears pushed out of her eyes. She looked up at her mother and sobbed. "Where's Sandy?" Her mother didn't answer. "Sandy," she screamed. "Sandy!"

Her mother looked at her for the first time since they'd been outside, standing motionless in the wet grass. She even smiled. "Don't worry, honey," she said. "Dogs are smart."

"Sandy! Sandy!" Meg kept up her wail until Sandy, head down and hunched over, came slowly from behind the shed. Meg yanked her hand from her mother's and ran toward her friend who looked up to see her and limped toward her, red gash on her blonde coat and small wag in her tail.

Driving to Iowa During the Flood

Rain sheeted from a bruised
And brooding sky. Flares hissed
The traffic into a single lane, as men
In yellow raincoats piled sandbags
At the highway's edge.
Drivers slowed their cars to watch,
But troopers in day-glo ponchos
Motioned us onward.

Beyond the turn, the river, black and frothy,
Poured over bags stacked twenty high.
A snake swam among the stalks of corn
I took for safety, but finally saw
Were only six rows deep, and losing ground.

Families in johnboats behind the wall of sandbags
Outpaced my car. Women in housecoats
Held their heads and wept, as dogs
Stood dumbly at the prow.
And everywhere, the smell of smoke and rot.

A farmhouse in a water field
Stared—dazzled—at the drowning trees.
Lights on and empty.

Anene Tressler-Hauschultz

THE LEVEE

ROBERTA SCHWINKE

Angie had traced her ancestors all the way from the British Isles. As an indentured servant, the first Obadiah McNeal had crossed the Atlantic in 1763. Gaining his freedom from servitude, McNeal fought in the Revolutionary War for the freedom of his new country. The McNeal family then took the westward way with many of their countrymen; first to Ohio, then Kentucky and finally Missouri, leaving descendants and kinfolks all along the way.

Angie was a great-great-granddaughter of the fourth Obadiah in the line. This Obadiah McNeal served in the 26th Missouri Infantry in the Civil War, being mustered in at Medora, Osage County, Missouri. Wounded, he returned to his wife and two children on the land he had claimed near this little town, but he died a young man from the effects of his war wound. The widow and children, one of whom was Angie's great-grandmother, moved away. Now Angie had traveled to Central Missouri looking for her great-great-grandfather's grave.

She went to the County Historical Society for help. "Obadiah died in 1873," Angie told them. "I have the government records indicating that a stone was issued for him and shipped to Medora. The grave must be there somewhere."

"Medora is in Benton Township," they told her. "We should be able to find the gravesite in the cemetery survey." But searching brought no results.

"How do I get to Medora?" Angie asked. "Maybe I can find someone there who remembers something."

"Medora is right on the Missouri River," was the reply. "And the river is so high right now, half the town could be under water soon! But we'll tell you how to get there."

Angie was determined to try to find the location of her great-grandfather's grave. Road map in hand, she drove the winding roads of the rural county. She almost missed Medora. Just a wide spot in the road, it boasted little except an abandoned railroad station and the Missouri River flowing wide and strong just across the levee. The regulars having an early lunch at the local tavern couldn't tell her much. One remembered that his grandfather had spoken of a graveyard where there were several Civil War era stones. "But I don't know where it was. I think it's gone now, anyway," Sam told her.

"Yeah," Ernest added, "it's a shame, but a lot of those old graveyards were bulldozed out before people got on this genealogy thing."

The guys at the tavern were more concerned with the impending Missouri flood than with Angie's questions. "With the early snowmelt up north, it will sure breach the levee."

The Corps has sent sandbags already. The National Guard will be here tonight to help us reinforce it," Joe, the tavern owner, informed them.

"It's going to take a lot of reinforcing," Ernest said. "Maybe the levee ghost will lend a hand."

"Levee ghost? That sounds interesting." Angie put aside her disappointment at her futile search to explore this new development.

"Oh, it's just an old legend," Sam explained. "People around here invent things for excitement. You can see we don't have much otherwise."

"I like old legends," Angie replied. "Tell me about it."

All eyes turned to Ernest, who seemed to be the old legend authority. "He's interested in that old stuff," Sam said, indicating Ernest. "He even belongs to the county Hysterical Society."

Ignoring the jab, Ernest spoke to Angie. "It's an interesting legend. For many years there have been reports of a mysterious figure seen walking the levee. It appears to be a soldier in faded Union blue. He walks along as though standing watch over the town, then disappears into the river mist. He is most often seen in times of trouble or threat to the town."

"Like this flood!" Angie exclaimed eagerly. "How very exciting! Has anyone seen him lately?"

"Nah, Joe has been more careful lately about letting people get too much to drink," Sam put in. This brought general hilarity, but Angie would not be discouraged.

"I'd like to stick around a few days," she said. "Maybe I could see the levee ghost. He surely is needed now to guard the town. Is there any place I could get a room?"

"Not much around here," Sam told her. "I think there is a bed and breakfast up on the hill. You'd be out of the flood water there anyway. And Joe here serves a pretty decent burger, if you're lookin' for something to eat besides breakfast."

Angie decided to stay, at least overnight. She was interested to see how the work to reinforce the levee went. Something seemed to draw her to this little town; the story about the levee ghost intrigued her. After securing her room at the Wren's Nest Bed and Breakfast, she wandered down to the river again. She could immediately see that the water was rising. A soft but persistent rain had begun. A crowd had gathered at the levee and a truck was unloading sandbags to be filled from an enormous pile of sand. As they were filled, they were passed from hand to hand until they were piled against the levee bank. In addition, a small dozer was pushing earth against what seemed to be a weak spot in the levee where water was slowly seeping through. It was getting dark, and lights from trucks and farm tractors illuminated the confused scene.

She saw Sam in the sandbag brigade and waved to him. "Howdy," he shouted. "Come to watch for the ghost?"

"It looks to me like there are more important matters than a ghost here," Angie replied. "Can I help?"

"Any help is welcome," was the answer. "We have people here from all over the county. Why don't you join that line over there? We let the person who is placing the sandbags drop off for a rest after a while, and everybody moves up the line."

Angie joined the end of the line and soon fell into the rhythm of the work as the sandbags were passed from person to person. Gradually she moved up in line until she was finally at the position next to the levee. As the person ahead of her showed her how to pack the sandbags in, she noticed that the levee was becoming really saturated and water was leaking through. She worked as fast as she could, hardly noticing what went on around her. Finally she had to pause to wipe the rain from her eyes. As she sank down on a sandbag she noticed what seemed to be the corner of a large stone protruding from the earthen levee.

"There are stones in here," she said to the person handing her the bags. "Look at that big one. That should hold back a lot of water."

"Yeah," her partner replied. "I heard once that they put a lot of stones from an old graveyard in here."

Angie suddenly stopped work as the import of the remark hit her. "Oh, my gosh! Tombstones? Here in the levee?" She reached for the corner of the exposed stone and began brushing the sand and earth away. Letters came to view and she excitedly continued to uncover the stone.

"Hey, what are you doing?" she heard someone shout. "Get away there! We're building this levee up, not tearing it down!"

"But this is a tombstone," Angie protested. "It could even be my great-great-grandfather's stone."

"That don't matter none now. We're trying to save our town, not going on some crazy ancestor hunt."

Angie ran her fingers swiftly over the now exposed lettering on the stone. "Obadiah McNeal, 26th MO Inf, Civil War," it read. She paused in awe a moment longer. She wished for a camera. Then she shook her head. "You're right," she replied. "This town is more important than any old tombstone." And she went back to furiously packing sandbags against the levee. She worked most of the night. Finally, toward morning a cheer went up from the crowd. "It hasn't risen in the last hour," someone shouted. "I think we have her licked."

Weary workers went home to bed or on to Joe's tavern to trade stories of the flood. Angie lingered with the few who stayed behind to watch the river. Maybe it was the excitement of the night, maybe it was the bone-tired exhaustion that she felt, maybe she drifted off to sleep for just a moment, but Angie had a distinct impression of a figure in faded Union blue pacing the top of the reinforced levee. "Good work, Obidiah," she murmured. "I'll leave you to guard the town, just as you have done for so many years. Your stone will stay here where you are."

Dust

I imagine a cloud drifting dirt, a giant
spiral of flesh over cornfields and rooftops
of corrugated paper. That as I try to
accomplish some small task – a cigarette
I meant to light, a direction
I meant to drive – dust whips the wind thick.
Or I water philodendron at my sink,
prune yellow leaves to trick death,
as silt crosses the floor in ripples,
as slowly the neighborhood, the street,
the yard disappear beneath this ravenous
shadow. I try to save
the rooms from accumulation, dust
which coats sills and spits through cracks
and chokes the kitchen. Then I imagine
the radio's instruction as the sheet
I've sprayed and wedged around the door
turns red with dust, with a fog that shallows
both day and night. I run out into the black
blizzard, where skin flakes and splits and eyes sting
with grit. The pick stalls and I'm stranded
on the running board of this gray
and formless mantle. And I quit all this
imagining and give myself to dust.

Marcus Cafagna

ARCTIC ARKANSAS

LINDA JOYCE

"I'll be home for Christmas." I sang to my parents on the telephone, letting them know my husband, "the boys"—our three dogs—and I would make it to their house in Florida on December 24. We hadn't celebrated Christmas as a family in four years, and I looked forward to quality family time as well as shucking my heavy Kansas coat in favor of a bathing suit.

I explained that we'd drive the F250 Crew Cab and pull our thirty foot, fifth-wheel RV we called Irv, since my sister's family and her dogs already called "dibs" on all the bedrooms in the house. Dad needed to measure the driveway to be sure our house-on-wheels would fit.

As avid RVers driving a behemoth and pulling a bus on our butt, weather is an important traveling partner, one requiring constant attention. Thus, on December 22, we checked the forecast for our anticipated route and methodically plotted our journey.

We left the rolling hills of Kansas under clear cold skies, crossed into Missouri at Nevada where the skies hung heavy and low, then headed south on Highway 71 dreaming of white. No, not snow. Sand.

The Weather Channel announced with their usual glee an impending ice storm in Little Rock. It threatened to shut down the interstate; however, not to fear, they advised that on December 23 skies would clear and people could count on finishing their holiday shopping.

And I believed every word they said.

At dusk, the rain changed to ice that pelted the windshield. When we pulled in to Alma, Arkansas, for fuel, a trucker confirmed the radio reports—the highway from Little Rock to Memphis had closed. Lucky for us, across the street, a KOA sign flickered on.

We spent the night in the comfort of Irv. Our own dishes, towels and cozy warm bed. The next morning, just as the Weather Channel promised, the sun was shining, temperatures rose, and we started the next leg of our journey—Little Rock bound. I called home to assure the family that we'd keep to our schedule. We'd be home for Christmas.

"Leave the lights on," I joked referring to Tom Bodett's outdated Motel 6 commercials.

We pulled onto the interstate at 9:00 a.m. and passed a sign that read: Little Rock 142 miles. My husband crooned with Willie Nelson, singing, "On the Road Again." However, before he could finish the last chorus, two lines of traffic that should have been traveling seventy miles per hour came to a grinding halt. Trucks and cars and RVs made a parking lot of the interstate. We were stopped next to a sign that read: Minimum speed 40.

And we waited.

And we waited.

A tortoise and a snail, if they could have survived the cold, could have made it to Little Rock before dark. We, however, did not.

Then, the slush the shining sun had created on the blacktop interstate turned to glistening ice as the sun went down.

And we waited.

And we waited.

Only not without calling 911 and asking what we should do.

"The sides of the roads are littered with accidents and tractor trailers have jackknifed," the operator told my husband. "Don't worry, we'll get ya'll moved by morning."

"Morning!" I cried. "Tomorrow is Christmas Eve. If we don't get out of here before then, we'll miss Christmas completely."

Not willing to wait on 911 to remedy the dire situation, my husband climbed out of the truck, carefully navigated the slick ice to turn on Irv's running lights, then he cranked up the heater. He donned his hunting boots to brave the below-freezing weather, made colder still by a stiff wind, to knock on car windows inviting folks into Irv to use the restroom and offering them food and water.

Time ticked away. The two-hour trip from Alma to Little Rock took sixteen hours. At one point, we sat in the same spot for over six hours in complete violation of the Interstate 40 mph minimum speed law.

Lesson learned? If you travel through Arkansas in winter, bring your white with you. No, not sand. Salt. The National Weather Service reports that icing is not uncommon during any Arkansas winter, yet their DOT hasn't the necessary tools to battle the conditions...unless you consider men who could be mistaken for Michelin Men, toting five gallon buckets of sand and spreading it like a turn-of-the-century farmer scattered seeds, as the proper way to handle elements.

We made it home just in time for Christmas dinner. Salt was on the table.

THE BLIZZARD AND THE BABY

CYNTHIA REEG

The howling wind rattled the store glass. I strained to hear my brother Dan's words.

"The weatherman finally got one right." Dan slammed shut the filling station door and brushed the snow from his mop of wavy brown hair.

"Yep," I said. "He predicted a February blizzard for the record book." I'd show him I paid attention too.

Four years older than me, Dan always liked to best me. But at eighteen, I was no slouch. After school, I drove our dad's bulk delivery truck to the local farms to fuel up their stoves. I'd just returned from my Saturday deliveries.

"Good thing I chained up the truck's tires before I headed out, or I'd most likely have ended up in a ditch."

Dan jabbed my arm. "I'm surprised you didn't anyway."

"Hey, I'd like to see you drive in this. That wind is roaring right out of the Arctic. Flakes flying so fast and furious it was near impossible to make out the road."

"Dad said to lock things up." Dan punched the cash register button and popped open the drawer to count the money. "Nobody in Zurich will be out in this mess."

Once Zurich was known as "The Gateway to the Northwest Wheat Belt of Kansas." In 1887, the Union Pacific Railroad ran four trains a day through it. Before my time, there were three grocery stores, two grain elevators, three gas stations, a bank, a lumberyard, and a café. Now in 1958, just a freight train and the jitney to Plainville ran most days. Only one grocery store, one grain elevator, our gas station, a post office, and two churches were left. On a crowded day, there were two hundred residents—if you counted the cats and dogs.

Zurich was seven miles, east or west, from the nearest towns along Kansas State Highway 9. Palco, where I attended high school, was to the west. Plainville, with the closest hospital, was to the east. Only a few farms and a handful of oil wells lay in-between.

"Ralph, look at that," said Dan. "Snow's up to the window-sill."

I peered through the frosty panes. Waist-high drifts edged the Main Street buildings.

"We better head home." I tugged on my wet galoshes. "Those two blocks are gonna seem like ten."

I'd already parked the truck in the grease room to keep it warm enough to start tomorrow. But as Dan jammed his wool hat on his head, a hatless young man barged through the door.

"I need help," he puffed. Mini-icicles clung to his hair. His shoulders wore a layer of snow. His breath came in gasps.

"Gotta get my wife to Plainville. To the hospital."

Dan and I looked at each other. We knew the phone lines were down. And most likely no other vehicle except our delivery truck could navigate the seven-mile stretch between here and the hospital in these conditions.

"My wife and her mother are in our car. We made it this far from Palco, but I ran us into the ditch just up the road." He grabbed hold of my arm. "You gotta help us. She's having our baby!"

Dan pulled the truck keys from the nail by the grease room door. His eyes caught mine. "Let's go."

How could we make it to Plainville now? It was four o'clock and nearly dark. I'd barely made it back to the station during the daylight.

Still, I nodded and helped Dan maneuver the truck from the garage. I scooped away shovelfuls of snow from its path. I put the shovel in the truck rack and climbed onto the left running board. The father-to-be clung onto the right side. Even with the wipers on full force and the lights on bright, Dan couldn't see ten feet ahead of the truck. Amid swirling snow, I called directions through the open window.

"There. Twenty feet on. I see them. Watch out! Stay straight. You're too close to the edge."

"The truck is slipping all over," said Dan. His gloved hands clenched the wheel like they were welded to it.

"Stop! Stop!" yelled the husband.

Dan pumped the brake. The truck skidded to a crunching stop about six feet past the ditched car. The husband jumped down. He tugged open the car door and lifted his wife out. She was a mite of a thing, moaning to beat all. A middle-aged woman crawled from the other side. She wore a hat pulled low and a scarf swirled high. She hugged her overcoat close as she climbed into the cab after her daughter.

"Go on," I yelled through the open driver's window. Dan shifted into gear. The truck slipped and spun but finally regained momentum. We chugged into the darkening twilight— a teen co-pilot, a nervous driver, a wailing pregnant woman, her worried mother, and a frightened husband.

The wind roared down on us. It blew gale force gusts of snow and ice. My fingers, toes, and nose went numb. I yanked my scarf up higher and nearly lost my grip on the door. I just needed to keep my eyes on the road.

"Watch out!" I called. "You're too close to the ditch."

"Can't help it," Dan yelled back. "The wind is pushing me into it."

The mother-to-be wailed louder. The wind swallowed most of her husband's plea.

"I can't go any faster," said Dan.

"I think we're about halfway there," I shouted.

"I hope we're farther than that," Dan answered.

Just past a derelict oil well, my tired eyes slid closed. Only for a second or two, but it was too long. Suddenly, a four-foot drift loomed in front of us.

"Slow down!" I hollered. "Go right! Right!"

Dan swerved. The truck hit an icy patch. The back wheels spun out of control. Dan pumped the gas pedal and fought the steering wheel.

"Noooooooo!" screamed the pregnant lady. She and her mother clutched each other as the delivery truck slid into the ditch.

Before Dan pulled down his hat, I saw the crease between his brows.

"Sorry," I said. "I didn't see the drift in time." I grabbed the shovel and jammed it into the waist-deep snow. We had to get back on the road.

I trenched around the rear of the truck. As I neared the passenger door, the mother-to-be grabbed her belly with both hands and moaned. I shoveled until I thought my arms would break. Finally, I cleared a path from under the tires.

"Give it a shot!" I called.

Dan gunned the engine. Again and again. The back tires, even with the heavy chains, only spun in the icy snow. The incline was too steep. We were stuck good.

A fresh wail pierced the cold.

I tossed the shovel up top. "We're gonna have to go for help," I said to Dan. I pointed to the women. "They can't walk to Plainville."

Dan climbed out and shook his head. "Don't know if we can either," he said.

We left the three of them huddled in the truck cab on the side of Highway 9. Dan and I linked arms at the elbows and bent our heads low against the wind. Still, the blizzard blew us over time and again. The fencepost tips, peeking through the drifts, guided us along the icy road. Numerous times the drifts were so high we had to climb on our hands and knees to reach the other side. By the time we saw the glimmer of lights at the edge of Plainville, I was numb from the waist down.

"Look!" Dan pointed. Two bright lights broke through the haze.

"It's the state V-plow," I cried.

With renewed spirit, we slipped and slid as fast as we could toward the plow. When the engine's roar drowned out the wind, we yelled and waved our arms in the air.

"What in the hell are you two doing out here?" asked the snowplow driver.

"We got an emergency," I said, barely breathing.

Dan explained the particulars. We climbed into the cab. The plow headed west. It took more than three hours to cover the three miles back.

"There!" I pointed into the spinning snow.

I jumped down and ran.

"How is she?" I gasped when I reached the truck.

The husband wiped a hand across his pale face and shook his head. "False alarm. The contractions stopped shortly after you left."

"What?" Dan's exclamation came from behind me.

"I feel fine now," said the little lady.

"Fine?" I sank into the snow. Dan dropped beside me. Sheer exhaustion pushed a snicker from my lips.

"Hey." I thumped Dan and pointed to the truck. "Want me to tell Dad you ran it into the ditch?"

Dan punched my arm. "Next blizzard, I direct and you drive."

I smiled.

Two weeks later the lady had her baby—a girl. They named her Danielle. I guess Ralphine didn't sound as good. Figures, doesn't it? Big brothers always get the glory.

Ice Dragon

Red-cheeked and fuzzy warm he
Lifts millions of flakes and
Smashes, crushes into
Artillery

Study Dragon's wide mouth with
Dagger teeth jut, gape
There's no going home 'til
He's safe

Frozen spheres fire into
Glittering maw, teeth
Break, shatter, fall into
White

She opens door, frowning, not
Seeing Dragon is now
Vanquished—he trudges in and
Smiles.

Rebecca Blevins

THE ICE STORM OF 2009

CAROL FISHER

In the winter when the weather man forecasts a snow measured in inches or announces the probability of freezing rain, folks head to local grocery stores to stock up on a few extra necessities—bread, milk, a couple of packages of ham, some cookies and chips—just in case inclement weather might force us out of our daily routines. We figure that by the time that extra gallon of milk and extra items are consumed, the weather will allow us to go about our usual shopping and food preparation habits. Not so when the Ice Storm of 2009 hit Kennett in late January.

My husband is one who likes to know what weather is coming his way in order to be prepared for our ever-changing Missouri weather. He kept watch on the Weather Channel when he learned that meteorologists had started predicting, as early as the weekend prior to the ice storm, that conditions seemed favorable for significant ice accumulation the following week. Consequently, he headed to our farm to cut extra wood for the fireplace at our home in Kennett. Monday, the weather forecasters fine-tuned their predictions, indicating the probability of a serious ice storm in Southern Missouri. By the next morning, ice was evident on trees, bushes, power lines and streets.

We had made our grocery store run, had the foresight to do the laundry, and had checked our meds and made a trip to the pharmacy. I had a pot roast simmering on the stove since early morning, just in case the power went off for a few hours. Thus, we could have one of our favorite comfort meals while we still had power, and before our menu was cold sandwiches. Proud of our efforts, we believed we were set. We felt we could relax and enjoy the warmth of a crackling fire in the fireplace, while still keeping a wary eye on the ice building up outside. We assumed and hoped that the storm would abate shortly. We felt we were prepared and would wait it out until the ice melted. Not so when the Ice Storm of 2009 settled in on our community.

Ice storm predictions were right on target. The rains came and the temps hovered at the freezing point. Rain continued to fall and thermometers displayed ideal freezing points. The rain kept coming and the thermometers refused to budge. And the ice continued to build up. We would soon experience the scope of an unprecedented weather event in Kennett, the worst ice storm in our history. Our power went out at about noon on Tuesday. This was the beginning of three weeks without electricity and cable at our home, transporting us from our modern conveniences to living conditions our grandmothers and great grandmothers used to talk about.

Since we have a fireplace, and some of our friends did not, we invited them to camp out in our family room when their homes lost power. We hung Grandma's quilts at the entrances from the kitchen and the foyer into the family room in order to keep one room in our house warm. Our guests "made do" by substituting our recliners, the floor, and our couch in place of comfortable beds back in their chilly homes. My husband and I piled more of Grandma's quilts on our bed and braved the dropping temperature in our bedroom.

We later learned that by Tuesday night our town of 10,000 residents was experiencing a 95 percent power outage caused by falling tree branches, falling power lines, and falling utility poles. At one point, for one hour, the power was 100 percent down. The icing event spanned forty-eight hours, bringing our town to a standstill. Fortunately, city authorities had sponsored "Event Training Sessions" in November of 2008. Consequently, they were able to quickly set up a Unified Command Center to manage efforts to address the disaster. By Wednesday city authorities established a curfew to be in effect from 6:00 p.m.

until 6:00 a.m. This curfew was lifted on Sunday, February 1, after power was restored to the hospital, Walmart, restaurant and motel areas. Our radio station supplied information with the help of a generator.

The Daily Dunklin Democrat, our local newspaper, was unable to print on Wednesday, but on Thursday came back with a Wednesday/Thursday edition quoting the superintendent of our City, Light, Gas, and Water facility. Addressing efforts to deal with the storm, he indicated that it would take "weeks not days" to rectify damage to the city's power system caused by the storm. Once the realization soaked in that we might be in for a longer haul on this storm, we, like thousands of residents in our community and in surrounding communities in the track of the storm, started to inventory emergency supplies more carefully, some going to other towns and cities to stock up on batteries, oil lamps, and generators.

Fortunately, temperatures moderated. Ice on the streets melted, but it was still winter and the damage was done. Neighbors reached out to neighbors in dealing with issues of food, warmth, and shelter. The Slicer Street Church of Christ, located in the vicinity of the utilities facility, did not lose power during the storm. Church members immediately started preparing meals for individuals and for linemen arriving to assist with efforts to get the town back to normal. The church became the location for Red Cross efforts and the VFW facility, a warming center.

Jim McCarty's book, *A Winter's Wrath, the Ice Storm of 2009*, details challenges that Missouri's electric cooperatives faced during ice storms. "Ice storms have taken place as early as October and as late as March. They have affected few people and as many as 500,000." He refers to the Ice Storm of January 27 and 28 as "one of the most damaging acts of nature ever to hit the state." He quotes Tim Davis, operations manager for Pemiscot-Dunklin Electric cooperative. "It was just an animal. People could look around and see it wasn't going to be a quick fix." Lines and poles could not withstand the buildup of, in some areas, up to four inches of ice. Power line workers arriving from Missouri towns across the state and from other states commented that the destruction they saw to power lines surpassed what they had observed in power line damage in the aftermath of Katrina, the destructive hurricane that hit the south a few years ago. McCarty notes that as a result of the Ice Storm of 2009, "More than seventeen thousand poles [over 300 in Kennett] were destroyed by the heavy weight of ice." In the same book, Governor Jay Nixon reported that the ice storm "caused more than $193 million in damage, [and] led to eight deaths."

Come late October, even though life has returned to normal, as temperatures drop and leaves begin to fall, damaged trees will once again remind us of the Ice Storm of 2009. We still remember the gun shot sound of tree limbs breaking away from tree trunks, the sound of droning generators in the crisp winter air, buzzing chain saws in the daylight, and the image of a farm tractor sitting in our neighbor's driveway, brought in from a farm—another way to run a generator. A large "X" placed on the trunk of a storm-damaged pine planted by our daughter's scout troop in front of their school about twenty-five years ago is a reminder that it didn't survive the ice storm.

We still recall the sight of rows and rows and rows of downed utility poles, scrambled power lines, and fallen trees yet to be removed leaning over rooftops and blocking side streets. We remember the tree trimming outfits who follow disasters arriving, eager to have a few weeks' winter work, equipped with chainsaws and bucket trucks and trained to create some semblance of order as they trimmed up, cut down, and hauled off the tangle and mangle of limbs and tree debris. Not to be forgotten were the long orange extension cords snaking through our house, delivering power from generator to electric skillet, freezer, and refrigerator, to hair dryer and DVD player.

We remember the questions we asked. Would our favorite tree, the stately gingko at the corner of our yard, weather the storm? Could the cypress tree branches survive the weight of the ice? And the dogwoods, would they bloom in the spring?

Bud Hunt, publisher of the *Democrat*, reflected in an ice storm summary edition, "The ice storm now moves into the history books. We'll be talking about this one for years, telling our children and grandchildren about how we coped: about cooking over a fire, sleeping on mattresses in front of fireplaces, cold-water showers. The ice storm will take its place in local lore alongside the other memorable events recalled as we gather with family and friends in the coming years."

And yes, our cypress survived and now is growing a new top. The sturdy ginkgo lived up to its reputation of longevity, and our determined dogwoods bloomed in the spring.

Storm Chaser

Wind whips, gusts howl, sirens shriek.
Thunderhead barrels and swerves up interstate.
Tornado drops, streaks across prairies, into towns,
flattens flora and fauna, peels roofs like sunburned skin,
splinters treetops wishbone-fashion.

Relinquishes its bully grip, roils the river and heads East.
Reverberating trees and strangled hearts, still.
Night air thickens, blackness sizzles with electrified ions.
People search for their candles and wits, survey the damage.
Worried loved ones contact each other.

My cell phone plinks a text received.
I read the message and gasp. My granddaughter,
the photography major, sends me a just-snapped image,
the swirling wide-mouthed monster bearing down,
chomping faster than her boyfriend can drive.

Her message: Safe. Isn't ths a grt shot?
I stomp and storm up the basement stairs,
shake the wrinkles out of my wadded up nerves,
send a silent prayer, "Protect those affected and this kid, too!"
I calm down and realize, I used to be young and invincible.

Linda O'Connell

A Joplin Tornado Experience

Brett Holcomb

May 22, 2011, started off as any lazy Sunday would. I woke up at a bright and early 10:30 a.m. with the intention of spending the whole day playing video games and dreading the next day of school. The day before, my family and I went to my brother's college graduation at Missouri Southern State University. The joy and pleasure that came from that celebration was still prevalent in all of our minds. Sunday, the seniors at Joplin High School were going to their graduation ceremony. Personally, I didn't know anyone who was graduating, but I was secretly happy that they were leaving and would clear up the cluttered school halls a bit.

Dinnertime rolled around at 5:00. We were eating grilled pork chops with cheesy potatoes. My stepbrother and his friends were out in our detached garage practicing with their band. At approximately 5:20, we heard the tornado sirens go off. My brother, Josh, was a bit of a storm chaser and was out on our deck watching the developing weather. He came from outside and told us that it was looking bad, but he wasn't sure why the sirens went off. I was still eating dinner, foolishly thinking that it would be another near miss that we have become accustomed to over the years living in Tornado Alley.

Five minutes later, it grew menacing outside. A friend of mine rushed outside to get my stepbrother and his friends into the house. Josh was back out on the deck, switching between there and the front porch, when he saw swirling low-hanging clouds. He ran downstairs and told us we needed to get in my room, which is partly underground and is the best spot for shelter. Immediately, the power went out. There were about nine of us huddled in my room. I did my best to lighten the situation with some humor, but we all went silent when the air pressure changed.

Our ears popped and we heard loud banging and crashing upstairs. Then, out of nowhere, there were ten of us in the room. Someone, Randy, we later were told, flung open our front door and sprinted downstairs with the wind rippling behind him. According to him, he was trying to get home when a power line fell into the street he was driving on. He saw the tornado shortly after, then turned around and looked for the nearest shelter. He tried our neighbor's house but the door was locked. Then, he quickly ran to our front door, and fortunately, it was unlocked. We later realized that if my brother hadn't been going back and forth between the deck and the porch, our door wouldn't have been unlocked. There is no way to tell, but my brother may have saved Randy's life.

We live near Iron Gates Road, and the last bit of news we heard before the power went out was that a tornado touched down near there. We experienced the weaker side of the tornado, but the devastation was no less traumatizing. Our first instinct was to go upstairs and examine the damage. Leaves and puddles of water were everywhere and the glass part of the front door was ripped out. Aside from that, there was no interior damage. Some of us went out in the driveway while the others went to the back porch.

Either way you went, it was like looking at a warzone. Our backyard had little-to-no trees left standing, and our neighbors were left without a roof. Over by Schifferdecker, across the duck ponds, as we called them, were houses we didn't even know existed because they were always covered by the shade of trees. Well, there were no trees, and all of the houses were practically demolished. The image of that hillside littered with debris, branches, trees, vehicles, and anything imaginable will stay with me forever.

At this time, the tornado was still on the ground but it was on the other side of town. I can't even imagine the kind of chaos that went on there. During the aftermath, we realized how insanely lucky we were. If you walked a block down the street, there were houses leveled to the foundation, or you could walk in the opposite direction and houses were untouched. We were right on the line of destruction.

For days, we went without knowing if our friends had survived the storm. We didn't know the path the tornado took until two to three days afterward. Our phones weren't working, and we had no other way of getting in touch with people. Eventually, we found out that no one we knew personally was harmed. I cannot stress how lucky we were.

The damage, the insurance company estimated, was about $17,000 worth. Two of our cars were totaled, and we sustained some damage to the exterior of our house as well as the detached garage. Our yard was covered with debris. In the week after the storm, we had numerous tree-cutting companies ask us if we wanted their services. Turns out we didn't need them, because a few days later, three different volunteer groups came and cleaned up our yard. For free. We couldn't possibly thank them enough.

My family was one of the lucky ones. We took some damage, but overall, we're like the other citizens of Joplin. We will come out of this much stronger than we were before, and we will be better people because of it.

Blizzard

The snow should have kidnapped us.
Barn-high drifts robbed Irish Joe of two calves
In his south forty and his Friday morning
Trip to town for booze and oats.

The winter deluge should have wrestled us down
Like Buddy Wilkins falling dead white, eyes glazed
Like nature poets shouldering guns
Only to contract buck fever
Despite the desire for that lean meat
That sustains through Ozark January ice
And ugliness.

The blizzard should have wiped out more than
Our electricity and extra propane and the neighbors.
That white-sanitarium-ward drywall
Hanging outside every window and snapping up dusk
Should have thwarted us.

You could say the firewood sustained.
All that chopping and drying and planning.
Buying ricks from Irish Joe
When he thinned out his north eight.
You could say that, but she wouldn't
Believe you.

Dave Malone
Originally published in Cave Region Review

UNDER THE ICE

J. B. (JANIE) CHEANEY

January, 2007. It came in three "waves," saving the worst for last. On Friday, temperatures dropped well below freezing, gusty north winds, thick clouds hanging low as a frown. On Saturday, you could stand out on your porch shivering in twenty-degree temps, watching the rain. *Rain?* Shouldn't it be snow or sleet? No; nothing so gentle. Raindrops froze at they hit the ground, and layer by layer, built up to the thickness of hand-blown glass, of windowpanes, of coke bottles. They froze on every exposed surface, making every twig a rifle barrel, every branch a cannon. By Sunday, the limbs started to fall: branches, poles, entire trees keeling over with a curious lack of echo—sharp and immediate as artillery fire. Like a whacked web, the power grid went down, the lights went out, the computer monitors fizzled. Then silence.

On Monday, the gas-powered chainsaws revved up and neighbors started calling. "Are you okay? Need a place to stay? Got enough water?" Surprisingly, we occupied a fairly narrow band of disaster: no ice in Branson to the south or Clinton to the north—but their Walmart shelves were cleaned of batteries and water pretty quickly. The widespread loss of power led to a boom in generators—and an unhappy little outbreak of house fires among families who didn't understand how to use them. Relatives, neighbors, and fellow church members got cozy as they moved in together for an indeterminate time—from two days to three weeks. A family we knew in minimally affected Ozark opened their home to a single gal, a divorced man, and a mom and dad with two small children, most of whom stayed for ten days. Unused fireplaces were swept out and stacked up, and families brought out Monopoly games and Uno cards for long games played by kerosene light.

The following Sunday, a full week after the storm, we wrapped in blankets and followed our pastor's sermon text with flashlights. "By the breath of God ice is given, and the broad waters are frozen fast... Whether for correction or for His land, or for love, He causes it to happen." Job 37:10-13. It could even be all three at once: correction, judgment, and love.

Correction: reminding us that our power and achievements are puny compared to God's, and a single storm can snap our strength like a toothpick.

Judgment: calling our attention to who really holds the world in His hands, and who must be acknowledged one way or another.

Love: it sprang up like crocuses from the inch-thick layer of ice on the ground. It sounded in every phone call to near-strangers, in the knock on the door, in the buzz of the chainsaw and the pickup truck loaded with brush. Crisis often brings out the best in us, once we have a chance to catch our breath and assess the damage and recognize how much we have to be thankful for.

Come spring, the trees remembered—acres of them with their middle branches stripped, putting out leaves so close to the trunks they looked fuzzy. Their tops sported tufted green pompoms like Dr. Seuss might have drawn. Every disaster leaves its marks—its sights to amaze. But the speed of natural and human energy to rebuild, repair, and replace is equally amazing.

SILVER STORM

BILL HOPKINS

The old man—now he called himself Virtue Longtime— hunched his shoulders against the bitter wind. He chain-smoked, watching people inching their way through the mass of trees felled by ice onto the road. Several of the people carried chainsaws. Others carried heavy ropes or chains. A few carried axes. All of them walked with their heads down, watching their feet, often slipping and falling. The ice was thick enough that even the four-wheel drive pickups required chains on the tires.

Such storms, called silver storms by old timers, were common in some years in the Ozarks. The sound of trees breaking reminded Virtue of armies firing black powder rifles, the reports booming in the distance off the hills and down into the valleys, soldiers in gray and soldiers in blue bleeding red onto the brown and green earth. The old man wondered if any-one in the crowd realized that they tramped over ground stained by the blood of young men in a brutal battle of a sad war. Virtue Longtime had been busy that day.

The old man consulted his watch, although he didn't need a timepiece to know that it neared noon. Freezing rain had begun before dawn and continued still. The sun's light, a sick yellow, barely broke the gray sheet that was the sky. It felt and looked more like dusk than mid-day.

Around ten that morning, massive oaks, huge maples, and tall pines had given up standing, their branches covered in coffins of ice, and fell as soldiers huddled on the losing side of a skirmish onto the highway running through the hills. For a half mile the road was impassable. Volunteers, unwilling to wait for the creaky wheels of government to turn, arrived on the scene. They heeded the unspoken call to aid their neighbors, a principle taught for generations by example and not words.

No one spoke to the old man. No one, in fact, paid Virtue any mind. No one bothered to ask his name or his business. For, if any of the women or men clearing debris had asked the old man his name, he'd have given them a choice of many names. And his business. He could've given them many labels for his business. The old man could've given them the information in any language on Earth because he knew them all.

His rheumy eyes shed tears against the stinging wind. Virtue wiped his cheeks with a large red bandana, peered at the end of his cigarette, took another puff, then continued surveying the people.

A woman, probably around thirty years old, although Virtue guessed at that since she was bundled from head to toe in insulated outerwear, struggled with her chainsaw. She stopped to tuck in strands of curly red hair. Once the machine caught and snapped and roared, she laid it against a tree's limbs, expertly pruning the limbs into manageable portions. Bark chips flew up in a spray heavy with the perfume of naked trees. The chainsaw cut the air, leaving an oily burning stink hanging above the people.

Two boys—hardly older than sixteen—slipped along the surface of the road, offering to carry the limbs away. The woman nodded and the boys loaded themselves down, struggled to a pickup truck, and tossed their burden in. All the people spoke in low tones, as if yelling would fracture the coating of ice that covered the scene.

A man, about the same age as the woman with the chainsaw and dressed the same as she was, shuffled on the ice to her and spoke. Virtue could hear the words.

The woman put her hands on the man's shoulders. "You cold?"

The man took off his gloves and touched the woman's face. "Amy, I'm cold as a black hearted banker." Virtue noted the man had a brown beard and hard hands. "I'm fine. Really I am."

Amy giggled. "Listen here, Randolph, my sweet…" She stopped, glancing around apparently to make certain no one eavesdropped. "When we get home, I'll warm you up." Her green eyes, Virtue decided, never missed much.

The old man smiled. *Young love*, he thought as he watched the couple hug. They released each other and fell to work, using a rhythm that said they lived this life every day. Virtue imagined Amy and Randolph on a farm, butchering hogs, planting corn, cooking ten gallons of sugar maple sap to gain a quart of syrup, sitting after a long day in the dark on the wide porch of a house overlooking a pond where tree frogs belched to their mates all night long.

It was time.

Virtue witnessed Amy slicing a branch that, after she'd freed it, slammed into her face. The crunching sound, Virtue knew, was bone breaking.

Randolph yelled to her, then rushed to her side. Amy sprawled on the asphalt, a halo of scarlet circled her head, pooling onto the crystalline surface of the road. "Amy." Randolph hovered over her. "Amy, say something."

Amy didn't speak. Randolph cried out like he'd been the one struck, collapsed to his knees on the ice, clutched his chest and moaned. "No," he said and fell across his wife. People gathered around the couple. One man, possibly an EMT, opened a white box and began removing bandages. Other than a man speaking into a cell phone, no one uttered a sound. A tall woman and a skinny man worked on the two victims.

Virtue stomped on his cigarette, glided to Randolph. "Randolph." The young man sobbed. "Randolph, stand up."

Randolph stood and stared at the old man. "Amy's dead."

Virtue held out his hand, palm up. "It's time for us to be going."

"Yes." Randolph touched Virtue's palm, then turned to watch the woman. "Yes. But my wife. My Amy. I can't just leave her dead on the ice."

"You can leave her." Virtue lowered his voice, although

only Randolph could hear him. "She's not dead. These people will tend to her, and she will heal. Her body will heal. She will be whole in the body but sick in the spirit and sad in the heart."

Randolph nodded. "I understand."

The dead learn quickly.

Randolph angled closer toward Virtue.

The young man spoke to the old man. "I don't want Amy to hurt. I want her to know that I loved her."

"She already knows you loved her. She will know other things."

"What will she know?"

"Your heart was weak and no longer worked in your body." Virtue pointed to a destination. "You will have time for grief as we walk."

"My grief soothes me already."

Virtue Longtime said nothing.

The pair of men never looked back as they trudged up the hill on the icy road, feeling the frozen rain encasing them, until they reached the destination, and blended into the silver storm.

Just One More Stick

We have a routine before going for blood
work. A place we sit and talk
about what sensations to expect and how
many counts for each breath
before the needle goes in or out.
Today, there is no routine
as we curl into each other and wait
for the sky to either rupture or not. Steady
whooping from sirens replaces some
of his concern, and all of mine.

He is worried about germs.
What may travel in
on the needle's sheath
as it breaks his thin veins.
He reminds me that it happens,
that people die from invasions
so minute as to be neglected entirely.
He reminds me that people disappear
in winds like these, too. There is indecision
in his brows—the stick or the green-black swirl—
which to command the worry
in this moment?

Softly he says it must be cozy
to be unborn, and I know this means
to wait without expectation as ants
must know heat through sun will point
the way up and out of their nested trumpets.
They nuzzle against the air's quick
rage with more patience than I understand.
There is simple comfort in such acceptance.

As the large capsules of ice collide
with every open object above,
I show him again, with the smooth rounded
cup at his feet, how to make a water ladder:
Take a finger and thumb
and lightly dip both into the cool water.
Then slowly push the finger
and thumb together, pulling
them apart in front of a wide-open
eye. Between his structure
of breath, concentration on frantic wings,
and mine, measured hums through noise,
he is pinching a finger to thumb
while he tells me one more time
that some do die, and that the water
breaks its bond too fast no matter
how gently he loosens the pinch.
I tell him, no. Not today. No, not ever.

Kelli Allen

17 Times 6

Spinning destructions
Arbitrary collisions
Cruel Brainless Beast

Know the way back home?
Formations fly overhead
Northward without maps

Cool one day, then hot
Not a question of preference
Sweat, shiver, write.

Be still Angry Earth
Emulate nature's pure grace
Imperfection's peace

Words rested today
The wind blew in from outside
Silently pining

Been on a whirlwind
The rain is steady gentle
Old friends come to mind

Christopher Limber

The Year of the Morning Walnut

When the breeze picked up, your ice encrusted
fingers snapped and fell in nested piles
around your swollen feet. Your crystal legs
shimmered blue, solid in both weight and cold.
You stood tall, as always, stately, sure.

When the wind metastasized, strengthened,
your arms exploded, shattered on the ground,
your limbs like glass, a fusion of wood and ice.
The torn hole at your shoulder revealed
the soft rot surrounding emptiness,
extended to where your breast had been
before that other storm, years ago.

When you didn't fall, I watched, hopeful
that what remained would recover, continue.
A year passed. I held you every day.

Then the world I hid inside shook in a war
of spinning and crashing, and you came down.
And finally, when I could reach the top
of your head, finally, when I could touch you,
you were not cold.

Rosalie O'Leary

Lucky Things
Melina Neet

The summer afternoon sky was dark. Marta had to do the dishes again. Cal, her mom's boyfriend, always did a search of all the utensils after she or any of the other kids did too fast a job. He found a fleck of something hard on one of the forks drying in the rack and told her to redo the whole sink load.

Since he paid the household bills while her mom was, again, looking for a job, everyone lived under his rules. No matter how dumb. Like the way he told her and her sister Annie they stomped and, with hands mincingly at his side, demonstrated how ladies should walk.

The absurdity of Cal giving them lessons on how to walk made them laugh, and he let them. Trying to predict when his mood would turn cloudy was impossible, so Marta tried, whenever possible, to steer clear of his nitpicking.

Today, though, put her in his path.

Marta plugged the drain and turned on the faucet. Shirtless, Cal padded into the kitchen. He had a short torso and long legs, so he always seemed to be propelling his chest like a banner. She hated his walk. He swaggered like a prizefighter who had let himself go soft, yet still proclaimed himself a winner, beer gut and all.

He took a glass down from the cabinet and switched the faucet to the other side of the sink. Marta waited while he filled his glass.

"Are you ma-ad?" The word came out in two syllables, his Southern accent derailing, yet outdoing, the tone the kids used when they teased each other.

"I'm not anything. You said to redo the dishes. I'm redoing the dishes."

"I don't think you want to get lippy with me, Miss."

She kept her mouth shut and stiffened when he swatted her. Cal swayed his thick shoulders like the victor of the face-off. Knowing better than to mutter under her breath, Marta kept her eyes closed tight as he returned to the living room. On Cal's Zenith TV, the baseball game was interrupted by a weather bulletin. Marta tuned it out as her thoughts grew as cloudy as the darkening sky.

Even before the dishes inspection, Cal had been on her case. She'd taken a cup of coffee up to her mom, and although she was in a hurry to get back to the story she was reading in the living room, she took the stairs as weightlessly as an astronaut. Cal's son, Wade, galloped past her and crashed out the front door without Cal seeing him. It was Marta who was summoned back upstairs and asked the location of the emergency.

Last night, it was her sister's turn to retake the stairs while Wade sat at his dad's feet like a lapdog.

In moments like these, Marta's mom would say nothing. Instead, she sat sphinx-like, drinking her iced tea and smoking cigarettes, her tan legs curled under her. When she wasn't tanning or filing her nails, she read Stephen King novels. Everyone in the house seemed to become puppets to Cal's wishes, Marta thought, as she watched her mom become a bronze statue in the background.

Marta had just put the last glass back in the rack when her mom came home from the store. Her sister, Annie, was carrying a gallon of milk and a plastic drugstore bag with a brown paper bag inside it. Her mom took the milk from her sister and told her she'd be up in a minute with some aspirin.

Cal came in as Annie brushed past him. "Don't let me hear you stomp up those stairs." He swatted Annie's behind. Marta saw Annie flinch, while Cal ignored both of the girls, his eyes fixed on Marta's mom.

"Marta, go get the other bag out of the backseat." She knew the explanation behind her sister's wan expression and the aspirin would be explained in her absence. As she shut the door, a siren sounded.

She came back in from the carport to the sound of Cal reprimanding Wade, who looked off in space with the absent look he affected whenever he got in trouble. He finished a Gatorade, swiping at his dad's hand ruffling his blond cowlick. "Marta, can you put the groceries away?" her mom asked as she filled a glass with water, swiping at Cal as he pretended to obstruct her. "Cal, quit." To Marta: "Why don't you start a salad?" To no one in particular: "I'll brown the hamburger when I come back downstairs."

The siren had ended, but now there was an announcement of tornado touchdowns in the area on the television. The station weatherman replaced the laidback sportscasters with his scarier intonation of "touchdown." Cal messed up Wade's hair again, and Wade yelled at his dad to quit.

Cal walked back to the living room to listen to the warning. "So are you a woman ye-et?" Wade used the same tone as Cal's "ma-ad."

"Wade," came Cal's voice from the living room.

Marta rolled her eyes at Wade, ready to flip him off. He got her in trouble for that already. Now he looked for every chance he could to make her do it again.

Her mom came back downstairs.

"Mom."

"Marta, I asked you to start the salad."

She put a tomato on the cutting board.

"I'm started. Is Annie sick?"

"Annie's not sick. She just got her period." She spoke lower, even though Cal was lazily yelling at Wade to get out from in front of the television.

Marta was resigned to certain unfairness. She would argue about the unfair things most remote from her until everyone laughed at how serious she was. The unfairness in her own daily life, like her sister, who was two years younger, beating her to needing a bra and getting her first period, just seemed like radio static.

Marta tallied the loss and began slicing the tomato.

A crash hit the front door just as the weatherman was listing new counties in the tornado watch. Either Cal had turned the TV up or the emergency people had a button where they could be the loudest thing in the room. Suddenly, the sky seemed like it would bend itself into the windows of the town-house apartment.

Wade was at the door first. And, Cal, pulling him aside, stepped out to look around. A tree limb, a thick one, had blown off and into the side of the building. Cal and Wade looked around trying to locate a tree with a missing limb. A human arm, one built like a machine, could have thrown the limb. The wind had gone limp, a shrugging troublemaker.

Their front lawn, and the half-dozen homes on this side of the development, overlooked the highway. To Marta, the horizon looked like a yawning and hungry mouth. Standing at the door, she felt an impulse to walk into its void. If this were a dream she could have, and walked out the other side, maybe, with the prizes bequeathed for surviving.

Marta thought of her favorite things organized in her bedroom. She had it to herself except when Valerie, Cal's daughter by his first marriage, came twice a month and took over, letting everyone hang out on her bed. Otherwise, it was Marta's fortress against Cal's attempts to treat her and her sister like he treated his own kids.

The wind was stronger now. It was an unseen hand pushing itself into Marta's face and blowing back her hair.

"Laura!" Cal called to her mom.

"What?" Marta's mom came outside, too impatient to stand with Cal looking at the sky. She had just started browning the hamburger for dinner. Cal wouldn't let her go so she pulled away from his hands.

As she walked back to the door, she heard the tail end of Cal's comment. "…good for getting that new car." In the six months since her mom had met Cal and moved their families together, Marta had heard Cal talking about being gypped out of his Cadillac when he hit his sales goal. He still walked like he was the champion of an undeclared battle.

He walked around the side of the apartment. Marta heard him call to her mom from the other side.

"What does he want?" her mom muttered, going out to the carport. "Marta, watch the meat." She did as told, crinkling her nose at her least favorite sight and smell. Her mom came in and mixed the meat with some noodles she'd boiled, and then added the contents of a seasoning pouch.

Marta went to the front yard. The sky looked lighter, more greenish. Far off, there were other sirens going off. On the TV, a remote voice announced that residents of the nearby counties should take cover. Their county wasn't mentioned. Marta wondered about retrieving her favorite necklace. Just in case.

Something lucky to wear if she had to walk into the void.

Tornado Alley

"Tornado Alley" is what weathermen
nicknamed the strip of land I once called home.
In Oklahoma, early spring was when
the rivers rose from their beds, leaving foam
and driftwood along their shores. They called
the clouds to share a drink, go for a spin.
Then Dad would yell, *It's time to go!* Winds squalled
through cedars, bent double. Within the din
we ran, our heads turned down, pelted by rain.
The cellar door was propped open to air
the cave below: kerosene lamp, a stain-
covered mattress, a moldy quilt, one chair.
My dad would wave his hands. Bird shadows on
the wall flew south until the storm was gone.

Linda Neal Reising

GEOFFREY

LYNN OBERMOELLER

For years my friend Dr. Geoffrey Hilton lived and worked out of his home as a chiropractor in Joplin, Missouri. Though almost eighty-seven, Geoffrey is healthy and active. He's also one of the most loving people you would want to meet. Geoffrey's New Zealand accent and lighthearted attitude always draw folks in, and everyone wants to be his friend.

When an EF5 tornado hit Joplin on Sunday, May 22, 2011, I watched the news in horror and worried about my friend Geoffrey. I tried to recognize anything familiar that might give me a clue about the location of Geoffrey's house as I nervously viewed the television clips.

With telephone lines down and electricity non-existent in Joplin, I started getting calls from friends wanting to know if I had Geoffrey's cell phone number. Since Geoffrey usually stays at my house when he comes to St. Louis, everyone thought I'd know how to reach him, but if Geoffrey had a cell phone, he'd never given me the number.

As my concern for Geoffrey grew, I decided to post a message on Facebook, giving his name and address, asking if anyone knew anything about my dear friend. I had recently vowed to stay off Facebook and cyberspace, and here I was on there more than ever. But I knew I'd find something.

Surprised by how many sites were already listed for Joplin and the disaster, I eagerly posted on each site about my missing friend: *Looking for Dr. Geoffrey Hilton, 1909 S. Highview Ave.* There was nothing else I could do.

I wanted to go to Joplin and look for him, but my husband discouraged me, pointing out the danger of people being in the way of professional volunteers trying to do their job locating missing people, taking care of downed wires, and removing debris. I continued to search Facebook for any information.

Monday I received a Facebook message from a mother and daughter who were Geoffrey's patients. Both were concerned about his well-being. They had visited the site of his home and business, and all they could tell me was that it was gone. My first reaction was they had to be wrong. They must have not known exactly where Geoffrey's house was located. It couldn't be. If Geoffrey's house was gone, then how could he have survived? My husband continued to assure me that perhaps Geoffrey was out to eat or out of town when the tornado hit.

Friends and I checked all the local hospitals and shelters and called all the numbers that were available for missing persons. I plugged Geoffrey's name into the American Red Cross website. Nothing. I tried later. Nothing. And again. Nothing. I continued to check the site and always, nothing. Geoffrey's patients and I kept in contact. They called four other outside area hospitals, but to no avail. Geoffrey's name wasn't turning up anywhere. The same patients went back to Geoffrey's house and searched under the crawl space and any other place they thought he might be. Nothing.

I continued to worry. Geoffrey had no family in the United States. I didn't know who would take care of his estate should something happen to him, so maybe it was God's way of making it quick and painless for Geoffrey and his loved ones. Can't go through any personal belongings if there are none. Nothing to sell. Nothing to get rid of. Nothing for anyone to fight over. I thought it would be a good way of taking care of things. I kept trying to see the positive in the worst—even if it was just in my head.

My heart ached as I'd watch news of the devastation. Tears streamed down my face. It was a good lesson in letting go—only I didn't do it so well.

Even though it felt like a week had gone by, the following afternoon on Tuesday, a friend called. "Someone has seen Geoff; he's alive and well."

"Really? Are you sure? Who's seen him?"

"Someone by the name of Lisa Barton."

"Who's that?"

"I don't know, but Bill," referring to another friend, "saw it and posted it on his Facebook page."

I searched Lisa Barton to find out who she was and what she saw. Her sister Gwen had seen Geoffrey. I was skeptical. I had no idea who these people were. I also didn't want to get my hopes up because of a false rumor. You can't believe everything you read. I had been checking other Joplin sites and noticed posts for people to be careful with what they shared and to be sure they'd seen someone, as they've had people find out later that the information wasn't true.

But thank goodness the news about Geoffrey proved to be true. I was elated and thanked God!

The next day the phone rang. I recognized the New Zealand accent. "I hear you're looking for someone?"

"Geoffrey!" I wailed in excitement.

He laughed and laughed. If you've ever heard Geoffrey laugh, you would know what a soothing sound that can be. My heart warmed hearing his voice. He then told me his story.

"I was standing in the hallway looking out the front window. Rain fell so hard I couldn't see a thing. My bedroom window imploded, and I thought I'd better do something quick. I was in my underwear and headed to the bathroom. I got into the tub and got as low as I could. I could hear the tornado, an unbelievable roar like jet engines right above my head. You just can't believe the sound. I heard walls being torn away from their base and floors ripped up. A two-by-four fell over the tub and then part of a wall, creating a tent over the tub. I waited it out. When everything was quiet, I pushed the wood off and climbed out of the tub. It was still rainy and cold, so I tried to find some towels to cover me."

As he talked, I couldn't imagine experiencing any part of that.

A Good Samaritan, Stephanie (a complete stranger to Geoffrey), offered to take him to her home in a neighboring city. She lives across from her parents' home, and they have a small trailer on their property. They hooked up water and electricity to the trailer so Geoffrey could have his own private space. That's where he's living for now.

Geoffrey is my role model. Despite going through this horrific experience and losing his home and business, I could see the smile on his face along with the sparkle in his eyes as he relived his experience while talking to me on the phone. My heart cries every time I hear the words that he finished his story with, "I'm so blessed."

Geoffrey's words are words to live by. Always feeling blessed regardless of your situation. I'm sure everyone who knows Geoffrey would agree, we are all blessed by the kindness Stephanie and her family shared in taking care of Geoffrey and opening their home to him. And to folks like her who have done what they can for others in times of need.

And we're especially blessed to still have Geoffrey for all of us to love.

Missouri Springs

My mother's birthday in May
rarely brought the corkscrew
shadow, Dorothy's conveyance
to land on a witch turning up her toes.

My May Day, May Day sent us
all to the basement, scoffers,
head thrown back, hands on hips
daring the sky, the same people

who never stop for the ambulance,
go for the green light against
the siren scream as if it is their right.
A microburst lifted our car

from the highway once without
a chance to run for a ditch,
my husband looking at his hands
on the steering wheel, unbelieving.

Shirley Rickett

THAT HELPLESS RACCOON REMINDED

HIM OF HIMSELF

HOWARD SIMMS

"*Distemper hits Festus area raccoons"—by Peggy Scott, for the Leader, Wednesday, Nov. 10, 2004*
The above headline caught my eye, and settling down in my easy chair to read, I found there were fifty sick raccoons in the Festus-Crystal City area. Fifty!

I'd hardly finished one paragraph before an image from the past flashed across my mind. I closed my eyes, leaned back and remembered:

It was a quarter-century ago or thereabout—a cold, rainy, fall day, as I recall—and the banks of the mighty Mississippi could no longer hold back the muddy floodwater. Water and flash flooding could be found everywhere it wasn't wanted. Low-lying streets and the lower areas of Hwy. 61-67, especially the crossing at the stoplights, were impassable.

P.P.G, the glass plant located near the Mississippi River, was not immune to the swirling water. The main plant remained dry, but other areas were accessible only by boat. Luckily, someone lent a fellow employee and me an aluminum flat-bottom rowboat with two wooden oars. Our assignment was to check the pump house that supplied water to the plant.

Normally, it was above ground—enclosed in a small brick building, reinforced inside with concrete walls. That day, only the roof remained visible. We rowed to the roof, cut an entrance hole and climbed down a metal ladder.

Water was seeping in, making it necessary for us to check periodically to ensure the sump pump continued to do its job, throwing the leaking water back outside. If the water level reached the low-hanging, 550-volt wires that ran to the large water pump, untold damage would occur.

My companion and I took turns descending into this buried tomb. It was a relief to poke my head out, climb back into the waiting boat and row ashore. Always, I thanked God for His protection.

The last trip of our pump house duty, my fellow worker pointed upstream, "Look, see that raccoon balancing on a floating log!"

I did.

The pretty gray and white animal with its ringed, panic-stricken eyes reminded me of a half drowned kitten. Its hair was slicked flat as the water splashed over the poor creature's back.

Then it happened. The log caught on a low hanging tree branch and twirled sideways. The helpless raccoon was swept from the safety of his raft and into the swift current. As he headed our way, he'd go under, then resurface—struggling, always struggling.

"Let's help him," I said.

"Are you crazy? That's a wild animal. He's frightened enough now. Hard telling what he'd do here in the boat with us!"

"But look what a valiant effort he's making. We're a long way from land," I said. "He'll drown for sure on his own."

My companion turned to me and shook his head in disbelief.

I did it anyway.

Just before the current washed him parallel to my side of the unsteady boat, I stretched out my wooden oar, the flat side up. The raccoon climbed on the paddle and crawled into the boat. The little fellow was happy to be there, but stayed on the far side away from us humans.

We hurriedly rowed across the wild river and to land— sweet, sweet land.

Me, I felt good, just the way I hope God feels as He looks down from Heaven and helps me out of my trouble.

And no, I didn't take that beautiful creature home with me as a pet. However, it did appear that he waved goodbye as he hopped out of the boat and scurried to safety, flapping his furry tail in our direction!

Safe journey, fellow inhabitant of earth, safe journey! God be with you!

First published in *Jefferson County Leader,* contributed by Verna Simms

Evening

The sun is setting beyond no man's land.
Eerie quiet settles over the path of destruction.
They sit on the front porch step,
stare across town, nothing to block their view.
There is no artificial light.
No sound of family chatter from porch or deck,
Or the cacophony of motors and horns in the distance.
Not even the blare of a TV.
No lawnmowers droning from down the street.
They sit, unable to leave because of nine o'clock curfew,
Stare out at a surreal landscape of flattened homes,
rubble punctuated by stubs of denuded trees,
bark ripped off by EF-5's twisting,
churning 200 mile-per-hour winds.
Is this what Hiroshima looked like?
Is this what Apocalypse will be like?
They wonder, hold hands, pray.

Bonnie K. Tesh

GALE FORCE

PIERRE J. MOESER

Cold water stung my face as I strained to see the lighthouse on Charity Island. Gale force winds whipped spray from the crests of the peaking waves. As the sailboat heeled hard to starboard, I realized that having ignored the Midwestern storm warning might cost me my life. Through the airborne spray, I saw that my course would take me past the north end of Charity and out into the middle of Lake Huron. My wooden 26-foot Lubec sloop and I would be no match for the storm's fury.

The wind shifted and I saw my chance. Easing the tiller toward me, I pointed the bow toward the safety of land thinking that if I ran aground on the north tip of the island, I could jump ashore to safety.

In an instant, I paid for my mistake. I had misread the wind shift and the boom swung uncontrollably to the other side. I ducked, but the boom collided with the right side of my head, knocking me down. I lay face-down on the deck, stunned. Though I knew the wind could catch the sail and capsize the boat, I could not get my body to cooperate and lift me off the water-soaked deck. Dazed and immobile, my mind drifted to earlier that day.

I had gotten up at 6:00 a.m. in Saginaw, Michigan, at my brother's house. He had invited me to come up from Carthage, Missouri, to visit him and sail on Saginaw Bay.

Getting out of bed, I stumbled downstairs to the kitchen where I found Jim's note on the countertop saying he had left at 5:30 a.m. for an emergency call at St. Mary's Hospital. I flipped on the under-cabinet TV just in time to see a report about a plane crash in nearby Zilwaukee. Knowing Jim's occupation as a trauma surgeon, I knew he was in for a long day, and I decided I might as well take our father's sailboat out for a test run.

After breakfast, I packed my gear and headed out to the car. Though it was past daybreak, the sky remained dark with thick cloud cover overhead. *A little rain never hurt anyone*, I thought to myself.

Though the wind picked up as I drove through the towns of Standish and Omer, I told myself that this would blow over. Grabbing a cup of coffee near the marina in Au Gres, I heard someone say that the dinner cruises on Saginaw Bay leaving from East Tawas and Caseville had been cancelled due to the approaching storm.

"Will be at least a Force 7," the man with the Gone Fishin' cap said to his friend with the leathery face and eyes permanently squinted from many summers out on the bay.

"No way," I told myself. Though I couldn't remember the Beaufort wind scale exactly, I knew that Force 7 would indicate winds over thirty miles per hour. I stepped outside the coffee shop and felt reassured. The weather report couldn't have been correct as the wind dropped to a caressing breeze.

As I headed out to my father's wooden sailboat, *Fluctuat Nec Mergitur*, I noticed a lone seagull perched on a buoy. On previous outings, my brother and I had been greeted by a chorus of squawking seabirds. There were no boats out on the bay, and I figured that this just wasn't the day for landlubbers to sail. Sure the storm flags were up, but I had sailed plenty of times in stiff winds on Missouri's Stockton Lake. I felt my confidence rise as I eased *Fluctuat* out of her slip, hoisted sail, and headed for the open water.

Cold water splashing over the gunwales snapped me out of my dazed reverie and back to the present. My body responded now to the perilous situation. I got to my knees and gasped. While I had been lying on the deck, the wind had snapped the mast off like an old twig. The mainsail and jib lay in the water pulling the boat over to starboard. A huge wave crashed over the port side, and I grabbed the rail and leaned my body far over the side to prevent the boat from capsizing. The wave passed and the boat finally righted itself, but I knew the respite would be brief. Waves continued to pound away at the injured boat. I tried to pull the jib out of the water with the thought of using it to capture the wind and gain some maneuverability, but I had neither the strength nor a mast to tie it to should I succeed. Another wave washed over the boat, and I thought all was lost when I heard a clanking sound. I looked down and saw a rusty Danforth anchor tumbling out of a storage cabinet. It would do me no good in riding out a storm of this magnitude, but I grabbed it anyway. The frayed yellow nylon rope attached to it bit into my hands as I pulled it out of the cabinet.

I looked up. I had just passed the northern tip of Charity Island, my last chance before being pushed out toward Lake Huron, hundreds of feet deep. I turned and looked behind me. A towering wall of water rose less than fifty yards away, and I knew I could not prevent the boat from sinking when the wave arrived.

I looked back toward shore in desperation and then, I saw it. An antenna tower had toppled from the edge of the island and lay stretched out over the water, half submerged. I knew I had but one chance.

I looked behind me again as the massive rolling wave gathered its strength. I spun the anchor over my head and flung it in the direction of the antenna. I heard the clang of metal on metal as the little Danforth anchor found the antenna, but I didn't have time to admire my success. The massive wave had reached the boat, and I felt myself being lifted as if I were on the initial ascent of a roller coaster. Not waiting to see what would happen next, I jumped astern and went airborne. I floated briefly with the spray pushed by the howling wind.

Once I plunged into the water, I kicked furiously to regain the surface as I pulled on the rope hand over hand, hoping the anchor had caught fast. After minutes of fighting the storm waves while my muscles burned, I reached the rusty antenna and pulled myself along the structure until I crawled, exhausted, onto the island's shore. I rested for several minutes and then walked to one of the buildings on the island where the lighthouse keeper greeted me with warm blankets and hot coffee.

Though I had survived the Midwestern storm, my father's boat had not. Through the ordeal, I gained insight into myself and the forces of nature. I learned to heed warnings and almost paid the ultimate price for the lesson.

Supercell

Did you think your life was straight as this road,
something that could be time-lapsed into a predictable gait?
Did you ever try to map lightning, predict when
the thunderhead would pause and fold in on itself?
Have you pointed to a place in the clouds and said,
"there" just before a ghost cloud twisted briefly into form?
It is all nothing, then supercell, multiple strikes through
the clouds while the tips of the grass shimmer awake.
From the deep blue that narrates your life
comes the pouring upward of white curves and blossoms.
From the dark, comes the thunder. Then the violet flash.
From the panorama of what you think you know
comes the collapse of sky, falling on you right now
whether you're watching the weather or not.
The world dissolves, reforms. What comes surprises,
motion moving all directions simultaneously, like the
losses you carry, talismans strung through your days, singing
of those you've loved deep as the blue framing the storm.
It rains for a moment in the field, in your heart,
then the weather stretches open its hand of life and says,
here, this whole sky is for giving.

Caryn Mirriam-Goldberg

Seasons in this State:
Zen Fails in the Heat/Cold/Wet/Storm

Missouri winter—
Ice sparkles.
From the ditch, I squint.

Spring in Missouri:
Red and green,
Like Doppler, not flowers.

Missouri summer—
A firefly blinks,
And twelve chiggers bite.

Fall in Missouri:
Golden leaves,
Wet, and I fall into

Shiloh Peters

HAILSTORM

SUZAN KLASSEN

"The radio warned about hail. Are you sure you want to stop?" Mom asked.

"It's not that bad. I'll be back in no time," my father said.

He dodged the pellets of frozen rain as he dashed into our tiny neighborhood store. I sat beside my mother in the front seat while we waited. Pea-sized hail pinged the roof. It clinked and dinged the car.

A few larger hailstones fell. A softball-sized ice ball slammed the windshield on the driver's side. The spot where it hit cracked into a jagged-edged spiral.

Startled, my mother flinched. "Suzy, get in the back seat."

A nimble child, I hopped over the seat and propped my elbows on the back of the front seat. I worried about my father. "Will Daddy stay in the store?"

"I sure hope so."

I squinted to see through the curtain of ice. Although it was afternoon, the sky was dark. The store's lights glowed through the front window. I could see movement inside, but no one stood at the windows.

Pings turned to thumps as heavier and larger hailstones fell. They pounded the roof and dented the hood. We didn't dare leave the relative safety of the car. Yet it didn't feel safe as the heavy hail battered the roof.

My mother worried that another window would be struck. "Suzy, get down on the floor and keep your head down."

I scrambled to obey. I kneeled on the floor and put my face on my knees. My arms encircled my head. The hail hammered and pummeled the car. Thud. Wham. Thwack! Nearby and in the distance I heard glass shatter. Bang. Crack. Crash!

Fear gripped me. I longed to see if my mother was all right sitting in the front seat. Determined to obey her, I squeezed my eyes shut and prayed, *Please make it stop.*

The heavy pounding let up. It returned to softer pings, then stopped. Off in the distance thunder rumbled, but the storm was over. It had only been a few minutes.

I heard voices outside the car and jumped up to see. The sky lightened. My father hurried toward us. He opened the door. We were safe now.

"Are you two all right?"

"Yes, we're fine," my mother answered in her calm voice.

Excited, I exclaimed, "Daddy, do you see the splintered windshield? Look how it cracked. It looks like a giant spider web."

My father examined the windshield.

"Do you think it will crack any more?" my mother asked.

He traced the cracks with his finger. "No, I think it will hold for now."

"But, is it safe to drive?" she asked.

He scratched his head, "Well, there's only one way to find out. I'll drive slow."

He turned on the radio and backed out of our parking spot in front of the store.

A reporter announced, "There's severe hail damage all over the city. Numerous businesses and homeowners have called this station to report broken windows. Power is out to several neighborhoods. We're tracking the path of the storm. Call in and let us know about your damage."

I turned to look out the back window of the car. Sure enough the store's front window was smashed. Someone leaned out over the broken plate glass window. Cautiously he inspected its barbed edges. The lights were no longer on.

I whirled around, "Will our house be okay?"

"We won't know till we get home," Mom answered.

My father took his time driving home. Large and small ice balls crunched under our tires. Debris from the storm was scattered over every lawn, broken limbs and branches, leaves strewn about. We passed cars that looked like they'd been beaten with a baseball bat. Splintered glass from the cars and the streetlights littered the street.

"I hope we don't get a flat," Dad said.

We passed numerous houses with broken windows. People outside checked for damage. Neighbors stood on front lawns. They looked stunned as they talked to each other.

We rounded the corner to our street and pulled in our driveway. Our house seemed okay from this side. My mother hurried inside with the few groceries Dad had purchased before the storm intensified. He walked around the outside of the house to the left. I ran to the right. I found the broken windows first. They were all destroyed on the bedroom side of the house.

The neighbor kids all came out. Together we ran everywhere searching for the biggest hailstones.

I called to my friends, "Look at this one, it's as big as the one that smashed our windshield."

A friend yelled, "I'm going to put mine in the freezer. The news station said they wanted to know who has the biggest hail. Wait till they hear about this one." She ran next door.

Another friend responded, "Oh yeah? Look at this one. It's the biggest one, bigger 'n yours. I'm goin' home to measure it." She ran across the street.

My mom peeked out her shattered bedroom window. My father looked down from the broken attic window. I studied their worried sad faces. To them the storm meant hard work and expense. To us kids it meant a contest over the biggest trophy.

Tornado Alley Is No Oz

Dorothy starred in no
reality show—
not because Oz
has witches and woe,
Lollipop Leaguers in
rainbow fatigues or bubbly
Glenda the Good, who
protects the hood from harm.

Dorothy dreamed. No real
Midwest twisters tote
farmhouses aloft
like champagne trays
in the Rainbow Room, no
cackling hags bicycle the air, no
shiny red trip-home shoes
await when you land
into the next nightmare.
Nothing rhymes.

In Tornado Alley, cyclones
bring buckets of broken
houses and hopes, rip
loved ones from families,
chop city lines to sadness.

Still—the people return,
retake the land of their great
and grand parents, the land
of their lives, their childhoods,
their first jobs, their last rest.
With tears and purpose, the people
rebuild, rehome, remember.
We, the people, come back.

Susan Swartwout

MY MOTHER AND THE STORM

LINDA JARRETT

I love storms, especially thunderstorms. I love the anticipation and the crackling in the air. The dark billowing clouds that pile one on the other, like pewter pillows.

Growing up, I did not get to see many thunderstorms because I was in the basement. On a humid day, the kind that yelled "Thunderstorm!" as soon as dark clouds appeared on the horizon, Mom would herd us to the basement where we would sit and wait for the winds to blow our house off its foundation.

That never happened, but Mom was not going to take chances. Once, I took my new portable record player, not chancing she might be right this time. No way were the winds of chance going to take my birthday present!

I wondered why she would always get so terrified. Granted, storms and their evil twin, the tornado, should be feared. But Mom's fear went beyond that. Dad and I would try to tease her out of it as we schlepped down the basement stairs, but that would only make it worse.

One night, I found out the reason.

The day dawned hot and humid—a typical mid-Missouri July. Before Doppler radar, weather channels, and twenty-four hour weather forecasters targeted counties and street corners for storms, those of us living in small towns relied on weather predictors such as flies biting and turtles crossing the road.

By late morning, the puffy white cumulous clouds began taking on shades of gray, and by late afternoon, the western horizon had turned from gray to darkest blue-black. The air grew heavy and the black clouds were tinged with green. The distant sound of thunder turned the day ominous.

Mom stood at the kitchen window, and twisted her apron. The newsman on the radio was now giving warnings about the storm.

"Where's your father?" she said, more to herself than me. Within minutes, he drove into the driveway and she ran to the door.

"This is bad, Eric," she said.

Dad hugged her and said, "We'll be fine. It'll blow over."

The wind had picked up, and leaves were flying off the trees, twisting to and fro. Distant clouds were rapidly heading toward town.

I knew what was coming next.

"We're going now!" Mom said.

I rushed to my room, grabbed some books, and was busy unplugging my record player when Mom said, "Don't worry about that. Come on!" And we followed her downstairs into the basement.

We didn't have a finished basement. No carpeting, covered walls, or nice furniture. Ours was a regular basement, dark, dank, a tad leaky, and inhabited by the washer, dryer, and shelves of stuff that didn't find a home upstairs.

I plopped down on the second hand sofa, while Dad took a chair. He turned on a rickety pedestal lamp and began reading the paper. Mom, however, paced, still twisting her apron. She started walking toward a casement window. She turned around; anxiety made her face a mask of fear.

Outside, the wind threw big raindrops against the window, and lightning found its way through the small windows. The thunder followed quickly, and we knew the storm would be on us in a matter of minutes.

I went to Mom and guided her back to the couch. Even though I was only eleven, she did not resist.

"C'mon, Mom. Sit down," I told her. "Storms always happen here. It will be fine."

She stared at the basement wall and murmured, "They aren't always fine. Not always."

Dad raised his eyes from the paper and looked at her. He opened his mouth to speak, but went back to reading. Somehow, I knew there was a reason for her fear, something besides the normal apprehension one has for a violent storm.

"What happened, Mom? Why are you this afraid?" I asked.

Another lightening flash, then a deafening crack as thunder tried to find a way to our sanctuary.

Mom took my hand, held it hard.

"I was seven years old," she said in a voice so soft I could barely hear it. "My friend, Molly, and I were at Grandma and Grandpa's. You remember their farm in the country? You were so young when we used to go there."

I nodded, visualizing the comfy farmhouse and barn where I had played when I was very young.

"The day was so hot, we decided we'd cross the corn field and go to the creek," she said, her voice soft, her eyes faraway as she pictured the field. "We waded and splashed. We kicked water on each other—it was cold and felt so good. She had this stuffed horse she called 'Rosie.' She'd dropped it on the creek bank so it wouldn't get wet."

Her voice lowered and I could tell she had returned to that long ago time.

"We didn't notice the sky. We were in the trees and it was shady. The sun could barely get through. But, all of a sudden, it was dark and the wind started to blow. Then the lightning started, and we heard thunder."

Her hand tightened on mine, and I felt her begin to tremble.

"We got scared and knew we had to get home, so we jumped out of the creek and started running across the field to the house. The corn stalks hit us in the face, and we tried to bat them away as we ran. I could hear Grandma's voice from far away hollering for us, and we ran faster. The wind blew harder, and the rain came. The lightning was flashing around us, and the thunder…the thunder was so loud.

"Then Molly stopped. 'I have to go back and get Rosie,' she said. I told her no; we had to get home. 'I'll be right back,' she said, and she ran back to the trees alongside the creek."

Mom got more agitated, and my hand hurt from her grip. Now the wind outside our house grew stronger, and a sudden flash of lightning with a resounding crack of thunder shook the walls. But Mom seemed not to hear. She had gone to another time to a memory that held her fast.

"I saw her running. I heard a horrible wind and saw this black cloud with a long tail. I didn't know what it was, but I knew it was bad. I couldn't run against the wind, and then I fell in a ditch. I was face down in the dirt, and I just grabbed some corn stalks. I heard a horrible sound like a train, only there were no train tracks nearby. I was afraid I was going to die.

"Suddenly, it was gone. I lay there. I thought I must be dead. I moved my head and started spitting the dirt out of my mouth. I rose up and looked around. When I got to my feet, I saw the corn in the field flattened. I looked toward the trees where Molly had run. Most of them were down; the ones that weren't were twisted, ugly and dead.

"I screamed for Molly, and I wanted to run to her, but my legs wouldn't move."

Tears rolled down Mom's cheeks. Dad had come over, and put his arm around her, but she sat there, her body rigid.

"Then I felt Grandma's arms around me, and Grandpa helping me up. I told them I had to find Molly, but they said they would find her, and they took me back to the house. The roof was off the barn, and a tree had fallen against the house.

"I was crying for Molly. But I knew she was okay. She had to be. She had hidden with Rosie. They put me to bed, and I just fell asleep. The next morning, I got up and looked out the window and saw Mr. Johnson, our neighbor, coming up the walk. I heard him knock on the door and voices talking very low, then Grandma started crying."

I could feel a tremor run through Mom and up my arm. She started to sob, with sobs so great they shook her entire body.

"They found Molly in the creek. A tree had fallen on her. And she had Rosie in her arms."

Mom put her hands across her face and cried like I had never heard anyone cry. I felt helpless, but Dad comforted her by hugging her close to him. She buried her face in his shirt.

I realized I was crying too. I wanted to help, but I knew there was nothing I could do. I stood up. It was quiet. The storm had passed.

Weather Tantrum

Thick clouds and wispy air
Wrestle in the heavy ceiling overhead.
On the ground, men with bald spots
Covered by brand name ball caps,
Stop their work and
Form a cautious audience gazing upwards.
Mothers call in heedless children,
Become vigilant sentries with
Knotted shoulders leaning hard
Against white porch posts.

Pushing and shoving,
Clouds twist and entwine
Until a cone,
Curled as a wire bed spring,
Drops down, pointed
Like a ballet dancer's toe
Reaching for solid ground.
Suddenly, swaying trees cease
In awe struck silence just
As sirens scream warnings of a twister.

Roofs tumble down the street
Turning cartwheels;
Fence posts bow down
To the cruel coil.
Then, after a quick assault,
Turmoil ceases.
Churning clouds move on;
The sky's seizure is over.

Families, like rabbits from burrows,
Ease out of fraidy holes
Scanning damage,
Measuring the weather's wrath.
Slow, intermittent raindrops
Fall from a bruised sky,
Moistening the earth
In tearful apology.

Claudia Mundell

A Silence

Once more, the aftermath: last week a line
Of winds leveled our town, clear-cutting trees
As old as Vigo County's oldest home;
Before, we'd lost a dying, bark-scarred oak.
Our other trees still stand. Amid the whirr and buzz
Of saws and chippers everywhere around
Us, Daphne and Apollo – purple ash and poplar –
Stir in the breeze, but stay unflappable.

Their branches arch above me like a nave
And now a silence spreads about: the wind
Animates the higher limbs, lifts them
Enough to let a slant of light slip through
Their folded hands and land on each green leaf
And me, the trees translucent as stained glass.

Matthew Brennan

Night Scene

It is night:
the ghostly gray foil of mist preserves
the fading freshness of the farmlands;
a gibbous moon short fuses the purpling clouds:
they wrestle across the southern sky
as two tomcats tangle in a time-forgotten alley.
The clouds are kneaded, twisted, their very quick
squeezed out in bursts of long, white spears
dashed against the earth and broken.

Phillip Ronald Stormer

TERROR UNDERGROUND

NANCY PEACOCK

"Chrissie! Come quick. Look at this."

Tim was in the living room turning off the television as I picked up my purse from the kitchen counter, ready for a night away from my farm. The television was making that horrible bleating sound when a weather alert comes on. *"The National Weather Service has issued a tornado warning for the following areas..."* I was in time to hear the meteorologist say that storm sirens were sounding. The radar indicated the dreaded hook signifying a possible tornado. Moments later he announced a tornado on the ground west of town and advised listeners to take cover immediately.

I peered out the living room window to see the usual thunderstorm clouds. Lightning flashed every few seconds. I couldn't hear thunder yet.

Tim asked if I had a flashlight.

"Why do you want a flashlight?"

At the look on his face, I found one in the kitchen drawer and handed it to him. He asked about candles and matches. I found those, too. He put all of them in his pockets. What was he doing?

"Grab your purse, Chrissie, and let's go," he called, as he headed for the back door.

"Go? Where?"

He looked at me like I was crazy and said, "To your storm cellar!" He frowned as he realized I didn't understand. "The root cellar."

I started to object.

"Come on! We're going to the one place that might keep us alive."

I was beginning to get frightened. The old lighthearted Dr. Tim was gone. Here was a stern, serious adult who was taking charge. Tornadoes were totally outside my experience. They happened to other people in other towns.

It started to rain a few random drops. The wind picked up. I heard clicks on the roof as hail joined the raindrops. The sound of the hail increased before we could get out the porch door. I thought of all those news reports that compared the size of hail to dimes or golf balls. Wonder how big these would be? Strange what thoughts run through your mind at times like this. Tim told me to wait on the porch as he ran back into the living room to grab a quilt. He doubled it over our heads.

"Hold this tightly over your head and keep it there. Big hail is dangerous."

He held me closely to his side so I wouldn't tread on ice and slip on the steps. Ice already covered the ground. Once away from the shelter of the house the wind drove the hail at a cruel angle, painfully hitting our backs and legs. I clutched Tim and the quilt. Why had we left the safety of the house to endure this pain? The quilt protected our heads but the huge lumps of ice slashed our arms. The pain was secondary to the terror. It seemed a long way across the yard to the root cellar. It was getting darker by the second.

"Hurry! Can you get the door?"

He held the quilt over us as I fumbled with the latch. I made my fear-clumsy fingers work, pushed open the door and teetered down the first few steps. He followed, closing the door. We stood on the step breathing raggedly, relieved to be in shelter. For a moment the thickness of the dirt walls and wooden door masked the sounds of the hail and wind. It was such a relief to be out of the storm.

I gathered the icy, wet quilt into an awkward bundle. Tim turned on the flashlight and helped me down the steps. He left it on long enough to light the candle, tilted it to make a puddle of melted wax on one of the shelves that had long ago held jars of vegetables and fruit. He held the candle in the warm wax until it had firmed. It lit up the small space enough to see the shelves and a bench for baskets of produce from my uncle's farm and orchard. He turned the flashlight off after checking the door.

"I wish I could secure this door a little more. It really isn't a storm door."

"Tim, I think there's a bar—a two-by-four—that fits across the door. It's somewhere on a shelf. I didn't throw it away when I cleaned this out. I never thought I'd need it. I wasn't even sure what it was for." I was beginning to feel a little more vulnerable as the adrenalin ebbed.

We found the bar and secured it in the brackets screwed into the door and door facing. By this time the hail had increased in size enough for us to hear it pounding on the door.

"There goes my new roof."

"I hope the roof is all that goes."

I was aware of the noise increasing outside. How could it get louder? The terror returned. Why did I assume just being in the cellar would keep us safe?

"It's so loud," I whimpered. I had never felt so helpless, so scared.

Tim reached over and picked me up and set me on his lap. He held me close with his arms around me. I held him tightly. "I'm sorry I'm such a sissy. This is awful."

"I'm as scared as you are. I'm glad your Aunt Lou needed some place for her canned goods." We had to shout to make ourselves heard.

We sat glued together as the volume of sound increased. We couldn't take our eyes off the door. I knew that outside that spindly door was death and destruction like I had never experienced. The walls felt secure enough to resist the force, but I had no confidence in Uncle Fred's homemade door. We could see the door flex. When the noise seemed at its peak, we heard a splintering sound above the storm noise. One of the wooden panels split and whirled away. The air pressure in the little room changed. The candle snuffed out. The noise that the door had masked came full force. We gasped as we cringed back. Was our safe haven to be snatched from us?

Tim picked me up and went to the far back of the little room. He grabbed the quilt and put it around me. Even that far away we were pelted with debris and water. He sheltered me with his body, pushing my face into the haven of his chest. I don't know how long we stood there.

As if someone had thrown a switch, the horrible noise was gone. It was totally, eerily quiet. In some ways that was scarier than the sound of the thunder and wind and hail. We both tensed, holding our breath, wondering what would happen next. Somehow we knew the worst was not over. The dead quiet was broken by a sound that defied description. It was all around us. The much touted "freight train sound" enveloped us. I couldn't believe the berm around the root cellar could withstand the force. You could feel it press against the very air inside the shelter. I clung to Tim even more tightly. Seconds that felt like hours passed. Eventually the pressure eased and again there was that eerie period of total quiet. The sound of a gentle rain was almost welcome.

As fast as it came, the tornado roared away and was gone. Tim released his grip on me. The quilt dropped off my shoulders, and I let go of Tim's shirt. I listened to the fading sound and looked at this man who had saved me. What could I say?

"Thank God we're safe. But I'm afraid to go out." My voice was quivery and uncertain.

"Why?" I'm sure Tim thought I was demented.

"What if there're Munchkins outside?"

He gave me a big kiss and said, "Let's go see."

We went up the steps to peer out the hole. I helped Tim get the bar out of the brackets and together we pulled the door open. Debris had piled against it and there was ice in a drift that cascaded onto our feet. Tim reached across me and pushed a limb aside. A little twilight lit my yard through diminishing rain.

It was hard to absorb the scene before us. The house was still standing. Shingles hung down off one corner. My big maple was down in the side yard missing the house by inches. We tried to take in the scope of the rearranged landscape.

"Wonder why it didn't destroy the house?"

"The main twister missed us. This is just wind damage." His phone rang. "It's the hospital, Chrissie. Bad trouble in town. They're calling for doctors. I need to get to the ER right now. You shouldn't be alone. Come with me. Maybe you can help."

"Always the doctor first, Tim? Good for you. Let's go."

Harmony Tornado

I was too old to believe it,
when the wind started picking up
more than candy wrappers and Coke cans.
I thought it still had a long way to go,
but I could tell it was time
to roll up the car windows
before rain soaked the seats.

I walked down the porch step,
mind you, not running,
leaving the rest of the congregation
standing under the roof.

Before I had closed the door
to the passenger side of the car,
I was face to face with a swirling demon.
I yelled but there was nothing
anybody could do.
I was sure this was maker-meeting time
as I bounced from hood to hood,
Continental to Chrysler,
tossed in the air above the poplars
that were growing beside the parking lot
(but not anymore)
then dropped in the soggy ditch
as if I wasn't good enough.

My glasses were on the lawn
of the house across the street,
my Bible next door in the rosebushes,
and my wallet two blocks away
near an overturned mailbox.
I guess you could say
I was a man about town.

When the congregation crawled out
from under the heavy oak pews
everyone was shouting miracle, miracle.
All I know is next week
when I attend the Bible Baptist Church
I'm going to pray a lot harder
and listen to the Sunday morning
weather report.

Walter Bargen

An Ordinary Evening in Springfield

After the wind settled, neighbors stood on their lawns,
stepped into the streets, talking idly of a double rainbow
larger than anyone had ever seen. But there is no metaphor here,
not the calm after the storm, not the darkness before dawn,
not the voice from the whirlwind, not a reason for the flood,
not claims that would make even God ashamed,
not the words that turn to dust in our mouths,
and should. Only the prayers of the people turning toward
a future forever changed, absences that will not be healed
this side of the storm, tree roots that cannot be unspiraled,
dwellings that will not be rebuilt. Only a small prayer
that some year from now you will step into an ordinary
summer evening, in a neighborhood you have come to love,
with those you love beside you, to comment on the day lilies,
the crepe myrtle, perhaps the sound of distant fireworks
after a ball game, and think, *this is the kind of evening
he would have loved, she would have loved,
would have called us outside again to see.*

Jane Hoogestraat

THE IMPOTENCE OF RAGE

BRANDON BOND

There was a time when he scoffed at that dread word of nature's fury, *tornado.* The piercing scream of storm sirens were an annoyance to him, and he continually cursed them whenever they sounded. When weather reports interrupted his television programming, he thought only of his annoyance at not being able to watch his favorite shows. One time, a storm pregnant with such winds passed close enough by him that he was able to see it with his own eyes. He stood as a spectator, lacking only popcorn to eat while he watched the dark clouds roll by. His was an artificial security, fortified by false reasoning. The fact that the house had been around for a hundred years filled him with complacent security. He couldn't fathom a circumstance where his God would rain such hateful destruction upon *his* household, *his* family. The losses suffered by others were a distant and exoteric exercise; that was something that only happened to *others.* That was before *it* came.

Reports of the encroaching storm had filled the news for hours, but they were ignored. He had other, more important things to worry about. Even if it did come close, it wouldn't strike him. His children played in blissful oblivion, and his wife's trepidations were dismissed as needless worry. He lost himself in a DVD, since his beloved television was commandeered by meteorologists. Then the power faltered, and finally failed. The children became frightened, and his wife urged him to take shelter. The raucous alarms cried out their warning in the streets, but his arrogant defiance kept him from submitting. When he finally decided to placate his pleading family and join them in the bathroom, the tempest struck.

Sound and fury, pain and disorientation overcame him. It was simultaneously a moment and an infinity of moments. Gravity abandoned him, and his own home became his enemy. Trapped in a horrendous nightmare with no escape, he gave himself up to oblivion and lost consciousness.

It seemed impossible, but light soon returned, and he found, to his surprise, that he was still alive. This brought an autonomic response of joy, but this soon gave way to confusion. He tried to recall his immediate past, but found the memories frustratingly vague. In moments, however, they returned to him, trailing pain in their wake. There wasn't a part of his body that didn't hurt. The bitter taste of iron filled his mouth, the unfamiliar taste of his own blood registering. *Tornado.*

All of these things happened in minutes, and then he cried out in dismay as he remembered that he wasn't alone in their house that had stood for one hundred years. Choking in the strangling dust, he struggled to find a foothold. It took several tries, as he slipped and fell in the shifting debris. His surroundings didn't make sense. Where was he? Where was the roof, the bedroom, the kitchen, the…bathroom?

Fear gripped him as he tossed aside wood and plaster, cutting his hands all over again. How was he ever going to find them? He listened desperately for the sound of their voices, their cries, but heard nothing. After a miserable eternity of searching, he came upon the remnants of the bathroom. There was the broken toilet, the sink, and the bathtub they had used as a shelter. There they were: a lifeless heap of horror. His family had perished. *Tornado.*

He raged. He raged like Achilles at the gates of Troy. Grasping the warm bodies of his flesh and blood, he screamed in anguish and wept in frustration. The passage of time no longer made sense to him. Everything became blurred and distorted. He was viewing life through a dark mirror, and everything he was, everything he'd known, crumbled like the hundred-year-old framework all around him. By now the unfeeling terror had dissipated into the ether, as if it had never existed. If it wasn't for the bitter legacy it left in its wake, it might have been nothing but a nightmare. In that moment, he became Job. He asked his God *why* with every fiber of his being, and was answered only in silence. He succumbed to fury.

There, all alone, on a mound of devastation and death, one man left the ranks of casual apathy and joined the great mass of souls engaged in desperate combat against the blind forces of nature. There was nothing so cruel as to face an opponent against whom there was no hope of victory. There were no battle plans or clever strategies that would beat these forces, ancient as the earth itself. Perhaps cruelest of all, was the fact that these forces had no agenda, no motivation, and nothing to gain from the carnage they wrought. There was no sinister intelligence at work, only cold indifference. He raged, and so did a multitude of others. Their voices joined a desperate chorus, asking, pleading, and cursing. But the tornado did not listen. They beat their breasts and shook their fists, but nothing would change the outcome of the tornado's wanton destruction.

Not satisfied with Job, he became Ahab. He attacked the remains of the inanimate building as if it were a personification of his hated adversary. He beat his fists raw and tore his shoes apart, but nothing changed. It was both the end and the beginning of his life, and he would forever bear the scars.

*"He piled upon the whale's white hump the sum of all the general rage and hate felt by his whole race from Adam down; and then, as if his chest had been a mortar, he burst his hot heart's shell upon it." ~ **Moby Dick***

Screaming Woman

The screaming wakes us,
like a woman turned inside out,
torn limb from limb,
but it's the house,
groaning, shaking, splintering
and the furious tornado,
sucking away our home.

We hide
in the tiny basement office
under the stairs. She shrieks,
tries to discover us.
Old files and forms and ledgers
fly around us
like frightened birds.

I hold you, feel your heart beat,
while she tears the breath
from the house, from our bodies,
pulls vomit from my mouth
to whirl in a cloud over my head, then
sudden silence, as if my ears
are clogged with clay.
She is done with us; moves on.

We stand on the naked lawn
littered with splinters, smashed dishes;
the maple we planted when Charlie was born,
all nude and broken.
It starts to rain. Is it safe?
Can we ever be safe again?

Niki Nymark

In Remembrance
Plainfield, Illinois, August 28, 1990 (29 dead, 353 injured)

I don't want to remember
The wind beating up the trees
While warning sirens blared
And the sky washed yellow-green.
How Susan ran outside for the cat
Shouting for me to hide in the hall
And I stood sweating in cold fear.

I don't want to remember
The aftermath of being left alone
When Susan went to check on friends
And the still wind pretended innocence.
Police sirens screamed for more help
As I waited forever with loud nerves
And the phone line silent.

I don't want to remember
Walking down the littered road
To find my old school destroyed
And teachers crushed at work.
Driving by the big church
With its remains twisted and bent
And knowing the faithful died praying.

But I do remember
And whenever the wind grows wild
And seething dark clouds show their claws
I have no illusions
That I will see a rainbow
One more time.

Linda Austin

THE STORM OF LAST CHANCE

L. S. FISHER

Dasha twisted her auburn hair into a knot on the top of her head to keep it from sticking to her neck. She sprawled on the porch swing of the Kansas farmhouse, brooding. Although it was almost noon, she wore only a thin cotton nightgown. She pushed against the paint-peeled boards with one bare foot and used the momentum of the swing to stir up a breeze.

Logan deserted her this morning, the back of the pickup heaped with his belongings. He even took the beagle, Shorty. Said he couldn't depend on her to take proper care of Shorty since she could not take care of herself.

He had threatened to leave for the past six months. "Dasha, you need to stop drinking. Promise you will."

Dasha glared at him with whiskey-bleared eyes and said, "You know I never make promises I can't keep." She may be a drunk or alcoholic, but Dasha prided herself on her honesty.

"I've had it," he said. Those simple words summed up twenty years of hurt, anger, disappointment. His shoulders slumped and he looked defeated. Dasha pitied him. She felt bad for the rip in his jeans, his scuffed boots, his battered Stetson. Maybe he would find a woman who was younger, prettier, and sober.

She lifted the bottle to her lips and took an unladylike swig of Southern Comfort. Black clouds loomed in the southeast, promising rain for the parched lawn and a dust settling for the dirt road. Dust hovered over the house like a mist although an hour had passed since Logan drove down the lane and headed east on the highway.

Dasha couldn't remember when the bottle became her solace, a replacement for love. She had given up on life after the miscarriage, a son that was not to be. Then Logan gave up on her.

Ahead of the storm front, sighs of a southern breeze clanged the wind chimes reminding Dasha of how Logan had picked her up so she could hang them. "A storm's brewin'," she said aloud. She didn't even have Shorty to talk to now.

Lost in thought, Dasha stared at the impending storm but did not see it. The swirling clouds, streaks of lightning and thunder grumblings became backdrops to the drama in her head—Logan's laugh, his rough hands clutching hers, his strong arms wrapped around her, the heat that breathed through her at his touch. Logan had been her leading man since she was sixteen years old.

Hailstones pelted the house, but Dasha, sheltered by the porch, ignored the ominous flat hail and its implications. The wind shifted directions, and she shivered from the sudden cold draft. She took another drink. The rumble in the distance sounded like large earth-moving equipment. Dasha closed her eyes. Her limbs felt heavy, unresponsive, but the numbing effect of the liquor did not dull the ache of losing Logan—and Shorty.

The funnel dropped from the clouds kicking up dirt and debris. Dasha slipped into another world, another time. Logan's dad played the fiddle, and his uncle strummed his Gibson guitar. Dasha danced with Logan, and he whirled her around and around making her dizzy, but so lighthearted she felt she could float like fluffy clouds.

Caught up in reminiscing, Dasha dozed. Last night had been so traumatic she had not slept.

The old Ford bounced over the potholes in the lane. A box of tools fell off the back of the truck and thudded unheeded into the road. The pickup screeched to a halt. Shorty bounded out of the open truck window outpacing Logan in a race toward Dasha.

"Dasha, we need to get to the cellar! The storm is headed this way."

Dasha forced her puffy eyes open. "Why do you care? You could have been out of the county by now."

"Darn it, Dasha. I felt like I'd left part of me behind. I was on my way back when I saw the tornado."

"Tornado?" Dasha's eyes bulged, the alcohol induced lethargy replaced with heart-pounding panic. Since a childhood friend had been killed by a tornado, Dasha had an unreasonable fear of storms. The only time she felt safe was when Logan held her in his arms.

The suffocating air was dark and heavy, black with flying debris. Logan shouted over the roaring wind, "Come on, Dasha. We have to go *now!*"

Logan wrapped an arm around Dasha's shoulders, and they bent into the cyclonic gale, into a darkness that looked like the end of the world. Dasha's legs shook from fear and too much liquor. She collapsed to the ground while Logan tugged open the heavy cellar door. Shorty raced down the steps.

The pickup lifted into the air, and they heard a crashing boom as it slammed cab first into the garden. Boxes, clothing, fishing tackle, a dirt bike, all so carefully loaded into the bed of the pickup last night were sucked up into the funnel. A power pole snapped in pieces, the crossarms dangled from the power lines. The storm stripped siding and shingles from the house. The porch collapsed, smashing the swing and potted geraniums.

Shorty ran from the cellar and howled as he cowered against Dasha where she lay on the ground. Logan pulled Dasha to her feet. She reached out to steady herself against the bucking wind and saw the bottle of Southern Comfort clutched in her hand. With Logan's arm around her, the tornado bearing down on them, she flung the bottle into the darkness. She picked up Shorty and walked steadily down the steps into the cellar.

She and Logan crouched in the dark, his arms wrapped tightly around her. "I promise you—I will never drink again," she said. This was her last chance with Logan. She felt stronger and more hopeful than she had in years and no longer feared the storm.

Previously published in *Well Versed: Literary Works 2010*

Mine

There were thick oaks and walnuts, upturned,
their barreled lengths filling the field,

and when I walked among them the morning
after, I thought of mares and colts bolting

in the wind-swirled night, fragile legs
snapping, bones jagged as the broken ends

of storm-lashed limbs. But we were lucky,
nine horses out of nine, all bunched like cattle

in the far corner of the pasture.
They're fine, Julie said, *frightened but fine*.

I thought so too until I read their eyes,
and through theirs, mine.

C. D. Albin

Sandbags

Every day
The river rises.

Hope won't stop it;
Sandbags are only
A little bit better than hope.

Men and women
Fill them and carry them
To where the water seeps
Through the failing levee,

Carry them
The way a pregnant woman
Carries a child.

Bonnie Stepenoff

LOW INSIDE HEAT

VON PITTMAN

Another five-inch rainstorm rolled over the Quad Cities on July 4. The first game of a scheduled Sunday doubleheader between the home team River Bandits and the visiting Ft. Wayne Cougars ended in an instant washout. The second game never started. The upper Mississippi Valley had been like this for weeks in the summer of 1993. On bright, hot summer afternoons, massive clouds suddenly rolled in and opened up. Rain fell at an inch an hour. Then the skies cleared suddenly, in time for beautiful sunsets.

For Jordan Tull, the rainout meant another lost opportunity. He had a single and a triple in just three innings. Because the game didn't last the requisite five innings, his hits were washed away, erased. According to the statistics, the narrative of a ballplayer's career, he had had no hits for no at bats that day. And with Slocumb—who Tull had always hit well—scheduled to pitch the second game for Ft. Wayne, he lost a chance at another big game.

"All these rainouts are killing me," Tull said to River Bandits' manager Jake Gattis. Streaks come and they go. And Jordan had a great streak going. This season he had finally begun to hit Midwest League pitching. His batting average climbed from .250 to almost .330. Thanks to five home runs over a three-game series with the Peoria Chiefs, his slugging percentage topped .480.

"Just keep getting around on those inside pitches," Gattis said.

Tull knew that his career depended on his 1993 season. He needed big numbers. He didn't need rained-outs. In 1992, he had struggled, ending the season with a .265 average. The California Angels, then the River Bandits' parent club, seemed set to cut him. But over the winter, the Angels pulled out of the Quad Cities and the Houston Astros took control of the River Bandits.

The Astros talked Jake Gattis into coming out of retirement to manage their new Class-A club. Gattis had a solid reputation for developing hitters. He telephoned Tull at his parents' house, in Ellensburg, Washington. "The Astros always need right-handed power hitters," he said. "We're gonna give you another try, Jordy. But you need to show us what you got right out of the gate."

After catching his breath, Tull said, "Thanks, Skipper. I'll see you in spring training, And I'm going to get on that low inside heat." For many hitters, fastballs thrown low, on the inside corner of the plate—or just off it—are the toughest pitches to handle. Jordan was just learning to get his bat around on the inside fastball when the 1992 season had ended.

Over the winter, he went to the Central Washington University field house daily to work against a pitching machine and some of the school's pitchers. "Come in low and tight at least half the time," he told the pitchers. He set the pitching machine to deliver just inside the plate, knee-level. He had such a good spring at training camp in Kissimmee, Florida, that the Astros considered moving him up to their Double-A team in Jackson, Mississippi, before deciding to reassign him to Quad Cities.

Tull had no illusions. By the end of summer, the River Bandits would either send him to Jackson or Oklahoma City, or cut him loose. Class A leagues exist only to develop and judge talent. They do so quickly. A few generations ago, there had been career minor league players, men who couldn't quite get around on a fast ball, or pitch "in the black," but who compiled good statistics, pleased the fans, and helped their teams in the standings. "Those days ended back when the Dodgers went to

California," Gattis told Tull. "Now it's up or out. Fast. You're lucky to be getting a second chance."

"I'm not gonna settle for Jackson, Skip," Jordan said. "I plan to be in Oklahoma City, playing Triple-A ball, by the end of the season.

"Good. Aim high, Jordy. And keep working on that low inside stuff."

Tull started hitting inside pitching on opening day. And he just kept getting better. He hit well at home and on the road, especially in the small parks like Burlington and Clinton. As a bonus, his glove work improved. He was running down line drives and Texas League pop-ups that he had let drop a year earlier.

"When you hit, Jordy, everything gets better," Jake said. Of course, every manager or coach Tull had ever played for—going back to Little League—had said that. Baseball runs on its clichés.

Tull's worry about not moving up eased off. His nightmares, in which he wandered around used car lots, never finding a way out, eased off. But he knew that streaks come and go. He needed every hit he could get while he had a hot hand. To stop hitting, to fall into a serious slump, would end his life as a professional ballplayer.

The freaky storms continued to hit the area two or three times a week. The skies opened and two-to-four inches of rain fell on the soaked fields and woods of Iowa and Illinois. The Mississippi River soon exceeded flood stage. Rock Island, Moline, and East Moline, on the Illinois side, had long since built concrete floodwalls. But in Bettendorf and Davenport, on the Iowa side, the river quickly overflowed its banks, in spite of sandbag barriers hastily thrown up by city workers, National Guard troops, and convicts. Within a few days, John O'Donnell Stadium, Davenport's wonderful 1930s-era ballpark, and the River Bandits' venue, sat in water up to its fence tops and into the second level of the grandstand.

The River Bandits' management had to figure out how to complete the season. First, they played a couple of home series at one of the local high school parks. A few fans, maybe one hundred a game, showed up with lawn chairs and coolers. With the rough infields and short fences, most of the players fattened up their batting averages and their home run counts. The total runs per game averaged almost twenty. Jordan excelled, with eight homers and eighteen total hits over a half-dozen games.

Then the team and the league changed strategies. The River Bandits became the orphans of the Midwest League, playing the remainder of the season entirely on the road, in the other teams' parks.

When the permanent road trip began, Tull's hitting started falling off for no apparent reason. He went zero-for-four on two straight nights in Cedar Rapids. After a decent stand in Rockford, he went hitless in four games at Kane County. His hopes rose at Beloit, where he got three hits, including a homer, in a double-header. Then the bottom fell out. Tull skidded into a full-blown slump.

"Skip, you gotta get me out of here," Jordan told Jake Gattis before a day game in Waterloo.

Gattis stared toward the outfield wall. "How am I going to do that?"

"The Jackson club is making a run for the pennant down there. They could use an extra bat down the stretch."

"Jordy," Gattis said, "the season ain't over here. If Houston wants you at Jackson, they'll tell both of us. You know how it works."

Tull wiped his bat handle on a tar rag. "I *do* know how it works. My average and home-run count still look okay, but they won't for long. I know I could hit if I could just get out of here. This place is depressing as hell. Everywhere we go, nobody talks about anything but storms and the flood. Even the towns with dry ballparks have had a lot of property and crop damage. If I can't get out of here, I'm done."

Gattis was used to ballplayers becoming desperate, irrational, and impossible to reason with when they went into hitting slumps. He considered telling Tull just how little most people care about baseball when their houses are floating down the Mississippi, or when the places they worked suddenly close, maybe for good. He couldn't say that, though. Professional baseball players had as much to lose as any homeowner or businessperson along the river. Indeed, those folks might be able to make a comeback when the waters receded. Struggling ballplayers probably wouldn't.

Avoiding the word "slump," Gattis said, "Streaks come and streaks go, Jordy. You just go out and play one game at a time and start the next streak. And while you're at it, move back off the plate about three or four inches. That should help you get around a little faster on inside stuff. Remember, the key is to handle that low inside heat." The best he could do was give Tull something besides storms and failure to think about when he came to the plate.

Jordan Tull hit four for four—with a go-ahead homer—that night. And the storm held off until the bottom of the eighth.

WHIRLWIND TOUR OF ST. LOUIS

ELAINE VIETS

I grew up in Tornado Alley, so I learned to recognize twister weather. My hometown of St. Louis has been battered by vicious windstorms these last six months. They seem to attack on holidays.

New Year's Eve, a tornado struck the south part of the city. Poor Joplin was also hit.

Good Friday, another storm stomped the St. Louis airport and flattened homes in north county.

Now it was close to Memorial Day. I was back in St. Louis signing *Pumped for Murder* and my other mysteries at local bookstores.

When I came out of the Borders near the Galleria, more grim weather was on the way. The sun was gone. I felt a cold wind under the heat. The uneasy sky was churning with dark, brackish clouds. Worse, long strings trailed from those clouds.

Tornado!

I high-tailed it out of the parking lot. I was staying with my friend Karen in a west county suburb. By the time I pulled into her driveway at four o'clock, rain pelted my windshield. The radio blared warnings: tornados had been spotted in the south, west and eastern parts of the metro area.

The TV was even more frantic. The weather map was dotted with tiny red twisters, purple patches for hail and dark green for flash floods. Those cheery colors meant misery and destruction. Between the local weather warnings, TV viewers saw the heartbreaking tornado damage in Oklahoma and Joplin.

By 4:30, the tornado sirens were wailing. Karen's lush green backyard still had smashed wrought-iron lawn furniture and two cords of wood from a tall tree that had been destroyed in the Good Friday storm. It was not reassuring. Neither was the sudden, deathly stillness. Now it was so dark, I switched on the lights. Karen's house has huge windows and no basement. I grabbed two blankets and the phone and shut myself in the guest bath, the only windowless room.

From there I called my husband Don in Fort Lauderdale. "There's a tornado coming," I said. "Talk to me."

"What do you want me to say?" he asked.

"Anything. I'm scared."

"I have good news," he said. "I don't have to work tomorrow night. Is your signing at the library tonight still on?"

It didn't seem likely. Jagged baseball-sized hail was breaking windshields in south St. Louis. People would be too busy calling their insurance companies to see me at the library.

Don and I talked about our work until I finally let the poor guy hang up. I realized my call was selfish: Don's last memory of me could have been hearing me shriek as I was sucked out of Karen's house. I figured that was covered under the "for better or worse" clause in the marriage vows.

By 5:30, the driving rain had slowed. My signing at the St. Louis County Library was supposed to start in ninety minutes. I called the library and asked, "Are we on for tonight?"

"We're in the basement," a librarian said. "We had to evacuate the building when a funnel cloud was spotted overhead. You can talk to Mr. B. He's in charge." That was James Bogart, manager of the St. Louis County Library Foundation.

The rain was easing and the funnel cloud had moved on. Librarians and patrons left the basement shelter. I said I'd go to the library in case some stragglers showed up, but I didn't expect anyone.

I was wrong. People started arriving at six o'clock. Old friends and new readers braved the flash floods and thunder.

James Bogart and the bookseller from Pudd'nHead Books carried in extra chairs for the crowd. By seven o'clock, some one hundred people packed the auditorium. Hail, tornados and flash floods don't stop St. Louisans. They laughed at my jokes and bought books. I hope the audience had as good a time as I did.

I left for Florida the next morning. I was in a hurry to get home to Fort Lauderdale.

Hurricane season starts Wednesday.

This first appeared in The Lipstick Chronicles blog
http://www.thelipstickchronicles.typepad.com/

Aftermath

Asphalt softens in sun
as another afternoon shimmers with heat
so intense that even birds can't sing.
The silence is more oppressive than the temperature
until a breeze begins to ruffle through starched leaves.
A woman lifts her eyes to see heavy clouds
blow helter skelter into a twisted thunderhead.
More twisted than the words spoken
before he left her this morning for another love.
The wind rises to whip through her hair
while raindrops slide tear-like to the ground.
But she doesn't move even when the heavens burst open
to release a torrent that pounds each blade of grass flat.
Her clothes melt against her body yet
she stands strong like the omniscient earth
undefeated and resilient as eternity
knowing life will bloom again for her...
after the storm.

Pat Wahler

IN THE BASEMENT

JENNY BEATRICE

The service was simple. Prayers recited, respects paid. It was all Marianne could manage. Besides, Eddie always said, "A funeral ain't bringing nobody back."

Mourners gather at the house as expected. Union men fill the living room and let the whiskey tell the tales of thirty years working the rails. When Marianne reaches to refill their glasses, they touch her hand and say, "Eddie was the best man on the tie gang," and "That damn asbestos." She smiles, and they are consoled. Their wives scurry about the kitchen, lining the countertops with casseroles they tell her will keep for weeks in the freezer. Marianne had readied for company as best she could, running the vacuum and putting out the guest towels, but with nurses on the night shift, insurance companies on the phone and Eddie on the respirator, she had let things go. She opens the kitchen window to let the gusts sweep away the stale remains of cigarettes and sickness. She notices night fell early, or so she thinks. She's been losing time and can't be sure.

The men listening to the Cardinals' game on the radio announce that funnel clouds are confirmed in Warren and St. Charles Counties. The distance from St. Louis is comforting, but the rain is picking up and the mourners down their drinks and move toward the door. They tell Marianne, "Sorry about the weather," and "Sorry for your loss." A few offer to stay. She assures them there is no need, and they are consoled.

The quiet Marianne longed for all day is steeped in Eddie's echo, so she turns up the radio. She tears out of her tight pumps and snagged hose, and flops deadweight on the sofa. The floorboards creak like the sound of work boots pacing off energy from the night shift, and she knows it's time to sleep. She drifts off for the first time in weeks.

A clap of thunder sends a shock through Marianne's gut, forcing her eyes open. The play-by-play she last heard coming from the radio has been replaced by the rattling off of the names of towns. She sits up when she hears, "Maplewood." The anxious weatherman tells her to find a safe place. "No such place," she says as she takes the routine walk down the rickety stairs. It's what Eddie would have her do.

She passes the clothing racks and old paint cans, and sits on the folding chair by the water heater. It's a front row seat to her wedding dress hanging from an old pipe, the one spot high enough to keep it from grazing the floor. She unzips the plastic bag that preserved the moment her heart was sealed with a kiss. The taffeta bursts out and it takes two hands to hold it up to her body, so much wider and softer now.

Wrapped in her gown, she dances her first dance, "I Can't Help Falling in Love." She feels Eddie's hand on the small of her back, holding her together. His hard-working hands were soft that day she gave her life to them. At eighteen her life was hardly her own to give, but one thing was certain—she couldn't live without him, and she didn't want to wait until she walked down the aisle.

"What in the heck you doin' here, Marianne?" Naturally handsome in his white t-back and suit pants, Eddie's every muscle flexed as he opened his bedroom window. She ran to him from her parents' house in stocking feet, forgetting her shoes and, as her mother said, the good sense God gave her. He smiled at the sight of her with giant pink curlers dangling from her hair and matching bathrobe sliding off her shoulder.

"Tell me it's true. Tell me that in two hours I will be Mrs. Edward Miller."

He leaned over the ledge, almost far enough to kiss her, but denied her with his sheepish grin.

"See you at noon, Mrs. Miller." He closed the window and pressed his hand against the glass. She ran home as fast as she had ever run, her robe flying behind her and her curlers flopping in the wind.

The hail pounds against the siding and Marianne gets one of her headaches, the kind that keeps her in the dark for days. Eddie had a way of talking her through them. "Breathe, like the train chugging its way out of the station, real slow." She struggles to find a rhythm, but every loud rumble breaks her stride, and she resorts to hitting her head with the base of her hand to knock the pain loose. Desperate to lie down, she takes the tools off the workbench. They look unfamiliar in her wrinkled grip, but in Eddie's able hands, they made a house their home.

"This place is going to need a lot of fixin'," he said shaking his head that first night on the splintered swing. "Even this dang thing droops to the right."

"In a few months when my belly starts showing, I'll sit my fat self on the left side and even it out." She leaned into him as they swayed under the speckled St. Louis sky, unaware that the swing was meant only for two.

Marianne hears the porch swing banging against the house, and branches are crashing up against the basement window. She grabs a flashlight from the workbench and sits on the concrete floor. She curls up with her knees close to her body and rocks back and forth. She leaves the flashlight off when the lights go out. She's become accustomed to the darkness since that day she was pulled into the spiral.

"I wish you would get that cough checked out," she finally said, after listening to the hacking since Christmas. "Your food keeps going down the wrong pipe or something."

"Maybe it's your cooking, Mrs. Miller."

As they laughed, Marianne noticed Eddie's favorite lasagna was more rearranged on the plate than it was eaten. It was the last time they ate dinner together at the table. It was a whirlwind, from the time they heard the word "mesothelioma" to the time they became residents of Barnes Jewish Hospital. The deadly brake dust that blew along the tracks traveled with Eddie, riding the fibers of his clothes and making its way into his lungs. It was years before the damage was revealed, and months until his last breath. At first Marianne clung to a hospital pamphlet that said 7.5% of patients in their early sixties will reach the five-year mark. At each consult, she held up the wrinkled paper and repeated this script of hope to the doctors, who would reply, "Mr. Miller was a smoker, yes?" and bury their heads in the chart. The chemotherapy was aggressive and Marianne held Eddie's hand through each treatment. It was the hand of a stranger, his thin, pale skin and his swollen fingers growing nails too long for a working man.

"How do you like me now, Mrs. Miller?"

"Just fine, Eddie. I like you just fine."

The nights Marianne stayed home from the hospital were filled with the constant ringing of the phone. There were the check-ins from the Voices of Concern, "Anything I can do? We're praying for you," and Marianne felt like a character in the neighborhood tragedy, told and retold on the barstools and at the bridge nights, the kind that make people hold their other halves a little bit tighter when they get into bed. And there was the stream of calls from lawyers eager to get Marianne the compensation she deserved. She never wrote down their numbers.

After weeks of biopsies, blood tests, side effects and disappointments, all that remained was "keeping the patient as comfortable as possible." And he was comfortable at the end, free from all his lifelines. It was quiet the moment the disease took the two of them.

Alone in the basement, she is surrounded by that quiet again. Everything is still, but alive, connected to the charge in the air. Free from age and ache, Marianne turns on the flashlight and runs, in stocking feet, up the rickety stairs and out to the porch swing and waits, swaying under a green St. Louis sky. The sound of her locomotive arrives. She closes her eyes and reaches out for Eddie's hand.

The Poetic Voices of Students

The youngest contributors to this anthology were sixth-grade students from Fair Grove R-X Middle School. These six students' poems were submitted by their Communications Arts teacher, Colleen Appel. Mrs. Appel is a teacher consultant in the Ozarks Writing Project.

The Editors

The Walt Whitman-style poems were written following a devastating series of tornadoes in the South prior to the Joplin tornado. Victoria Fishback recalled the tornado that damaged our own school in 2009 in her Whitman copy/change poem. The Joplin tornado poems were a result of weaving the words of New *York Times* reporter Noam Cohen with the words of Bonnie Tyler's song "Holding Out for a Hero."

Place-based writing is an important element of the curriculum at Fair Grove Middle School. Students write to discover our connections to family and community. Much of our writing reflects the concern we have for others. We are grateful that our words can benefit the students in Joplin.

Colleen Appel

Joplin Needs a Hero

Joplin needs a hero
to fight the tornado
that steamrolled over it.
It's gonna take a superman
to find the vanished people,
to fix the mangled destruction,
He has to be
fast,
he has to be
strong,
and he has to be
larger than life.
I feel him coming
like the fire in my blood.
Joplin needs a hero
and I swear he's watching
them.

Cody Sisco

Devastation

A tornado steamrolled over Joplin
I need a hero
late Sunday night
There's someone reaching back for me
Devastation hinted at the storm's power
Racing on the thunder and rising with the heat
Left isolated and in the dark
It's gonna take a superman
There was a panic
Up where the mountains meet the heavens above
Some just had blankets
I can feel his approach
Blown across the hall
Like the fire in my blood

Leah Wahlquist

Joplin

Joplin was left isolated and in the dark
They're holding out for a hero
and he's gotta come quick.
What were houses is now debris
It's gonna take God
to put them back on their feet.
They have nothing except the clothes on their backs, but they know
a powerful hero is coming back.

Hannah Mallard

Innocent

Joplin was left isolated and in the dark
Joplin needs a hero
to sweep up all this debris
He's gotta be strong
And he needs to come fast
because
that tornado steamrolled over Joplin,
a city with many innocent people
moving to Heaven

Hannah Fox

When I Heard the Stories
after Walt Whitman

When I saw pictures and videos of tornadoes in the South,
When I heard how many people died,
When I heard they evacuated some cities,
How soon will it be before their town is normal again,
Till searching and finding is over,
In and under houses under the rubble,
Hoping all the bodies are found.

Ryan Burks

Tornado Disaster
after Walt Whitman

When I heard the siren,
When our town took cover,
When I looked around,
When I finally realized we were in danger,
How soon understandably I became scared and worried,
Till standing and looking around,
In the remains of our town and school,
Looked and realized this is going to need lots of healing.

Victoria Fishback

AUTHOR BIOS

C. D. Albin teaches English at Missouri State University – West Plains, where he edits *Elder Mountain: A Journal of Ozarks Studies*. His poems, stories, and reviews have appeared in a number of journals, including *Arkansas Review, Big Muddy, Cape Rock, Georgia Review, Harvard Review, Natural Bridge*, and *Rockhurst Review*.

Kelli Allen is an award-winning poet and scholar. Her work has appeared or is forthcoming in *Poetry Quarterly, Puerto del Sol, Abridged, Gargoyle, The Blue Sofa Review, WomenArts Quarterly, The Caper Review, It Has Come to This: Poets of the Great Mother Conference Lugh Review* (where she was the featured author), *The Chaffy Review, Euphony,* "Tea With George," and elsewhere. She is the author of two chapbooks (*Applied Cryptography; Picturing What Breaks*) and has served as the Managing Editor of *Natural Bridge*. Allen also serves as Director of Development for The Missouri Warrior Writers Project. She is the founder and director of the Graduate Writers Reading Series for the University of Missouri St. Louis.

Linda Austin dabbles in poetry and micro fiction and is an advocate for life-writing. She is coauthor of *Cherry Blossoms in Twilight*, a memoir of her mother growing up during WWII in Japan. She has weathered two deadly tornados and one hurricane, and barely escaped from a dangerous snowstorm.

Walter Bargen was appointed Missouri's first poet laureate in 2008. He received a BA in philosophy and an MA in English education from the University of Missouri, Columbia. Bargen is the author of more than a dozen collections of poetry, including

Days Like This Are Necessary: New and Selected Poems (2009).

Jenny Beatrice, originally from New Jersey, has lived in St. Louis since 1999. She and her husband, three children, mother and family dog squeeze into every available square foot of her lived-in Webster Groves home. She puts her degree in religious studies and passion for writing to good use as the director of communications for the Sisters of St. Joseph of Carondelet. She is also the Web site coordinator for Walrus Publishing of St. Louis.

Rebecca Blevins lives in northwest Missouri, land of tornadoes and cows. (Hopefully not mixed together.) She began reading before she can remember, so books have always been part of her life. Her love of reading has translated into an affinity for writing. Rebecca's first book at age four was a huge hit—a cardboard-covered masterpiece with pages of stick figure drawings. Now, she writes about pirates with rooster pox and princesses with pet aardvarks.

Brandon Bond is a thirty-year-old Branch Assistant at the Willard Library, which is part of the Springfield-Greene County Library District.

Matthew Brennan has contributed poems to such journals as *Sewanee Review, Elder Mountain, South Carolina Review, Poetry Ireland Review*, and *Cape Rock*. He has published four books of poetry, most recently *The House with the Mansard Roof* (Backwaters Press, 2009) and *The Sea-Crossing of Saint Brendan* (Birch Brook Press, 2008). A native of Missouri, he teaches at Indiana State U.

Cully Bryant is a family physician and writer residing in Sikeston, Missouri. His writing spans many genres and can be found in online and print literary journals including: *Ampersand, Oak Bend Review, Illumen, Beeswax, Fuselit, Clapboard House* and others. His debut novel, *Messages,* is tentatively scheduled for release in late 2011 through Dailey Swan Publishing.

Kathryn Buckstaff is an award-winning journalist and author of books, magazine articles, poetry and short stories. In the mid-1970s, Buckstaff lived in Newton County in northwest Arkansas near the Buffalo River. St. Martin's Press has published her books: *No One Dies in Branson, Evil Harmony* and *Branson and Beyond: A Country Music Lover's Guide to Branson, Nashville, and Pigeon Forge.*

Marcus Cafagna is the author of two books, *The Broken World* (University of Illinois Press, 1996), a National Poetry Series selection, and *Roman Fever* (Invisible Cities Press/IPG, 2001). His poems have appeared in *Poetry, TriQuarterly, The Southern Review*, among numerous other journals and anthologies. He lives in the Ozarks and coordinates the creative writing program at Missouri State University.

Bill Cairns is a carpenter, and a member of the Society of Children's Writers and Illustrators. He lives in Ottawa, Illinois, where he has over thirty-four years' active service with the Ottawa Rescue Squad, a volunteer river rescue unit.

J. B. (Janie) Cheaney is a writer who lives in the Springfield area. She is the author of four novels for children, all published by Random House, a senior writer for WORLD Magazine, and co-creator of Redeemed Reader, a children's literature blog.

John Cunningham is the apple of his father's eye with a face only a mother could love. He is a student in a phenomenal M.F.A. program at Lindenwood University in St. Charles, Missouri. He wanted to be a storm chaser until this year and has instead opted for writing, painting, playing music, and the unemployment line.

Cheryl Davis is a librarian and freelance writer from Springdale, Arkansas. She is the author of *Cookie Boy: Travelin' Arkansas* which was recently awarded the Susannah DeBlack Award from the Arkansas Historical Association.

Teddi Doleski is the author of *The Hurt* and *Silvester and the Oogaloo Boogaloo.* Her work has appeared in *The Writer, Cricket,* and the Cousteau Society's *Dolphin Log.* She has served as writer-in-residence in the Arts in Education program of the Kansas Arts Council. She lives in Shawnee, Kansas and has great respect for weather.

Carol Fisher is in a second career as a freelance writer after teaching English and speech communication for thirty-three years in Missouri public schools. She has three books on food history and cookbook history to her credit and is currently working on a fourth. Fisher's credits also include feature articles and garden columns for her local newspaper. She is a member of Heartland Writers Guild, Missouri Writers' Guild, Ozark Writers League, and Missouri Folklore Society.

L. S. Fisher, Mozark Press, is the project leader and editor of the *Shaker of Margarita* series. She has published three books of essays from her award-winning Early Onset Alzheimer's health blog, earlyonset.blogspot.com. Linda has won awards and prizes for her stories and essays. She has been published in *A Cup of Comfort, Chicken Soup for the Soul,* other anthologies, and online publications. "Storm of Last Chance" won an honorable mention in *Well Versed* 2010.

Karin Frank's poems have been published or are forthcoming in the *Rockhurst Review, Taj Mahal Review, I-70 Review, Mid-America Poetry Review, Little Balkans Review, Coal City Review, Kansas City Voices, Asimov's Tales of the Talisman and Dreams and Nightmares* and the anthologies, *Cost of Freedom and Free Wheeling.* Her prose has been published or is forthcoming in *Kansas City Voices, Chicken Soup* and the *Shaker of Margaritas: Cougars on the Prowl.*

Anne Grady is a writer and musician living in St. Louis.

Dianna Graveman, MFA, is a St. Louis editor, writer, and educator. She has authored and edited many fiction and nonfiction pieces for magazines, newspapers, anthologies, and journals, and is coauthor of four regional histories. Graveman provides small business communications and editorial services under her company name, 2 Rivers Communications & Design. Visit her at 2RiversCommunications.com or via email at dianna@2riverscommunications.com.

Todd Hanks lives at the Lake of the Ozarks. His poetry has appeared in publications such as *Asimov's Science Fiction Magazine* and the *Kansas City Star* newspaper.

Brett Holcomb was born and raised in Joplin, Missouri. He has lived there his whole life with his family and currently attends Joplin High School as a sophomore. Writing, creatively and informatively, has been a hobby of his for years. He has one complete manuscript for a fiction book as well as several unfinished ones. He would like to be a published author some day.

Jane Hoogestraat was born in South Dakota and educated at Baylor and the University of Chicago. Her first chapbook, *Winnowing Out Our Souls* (2007), was published by Foothills Press; her second chapbook, *Harvesting All Night* (2009), won the Finishing Line Press Open Competition. In addition, she has published in such journals as *Fourth River*, *Image, Potomac Review,* and *Southern Review.* She teaches at Missouri State, specializing in 20th century poetry and literary theory.

Bill Hopkins is retired after beginning his legal career in 1971 and serving as a private attorney, prosecuting attorney, an administrative law judge, and a trial court judge, all in Missouri. His poems, short stories, and non-fiction have appeared in many different publications. He's had several short plays produced. He has also written a book of collected poetry, *Moving Into Forever.* Bill is a member of Mystery Writers of America, Dramatists Guild, Horror Writers Association, Missouri Writers' Guild, and Sisters In Crime. Bill is also a photographer who has sold work in the United States, Canada, and Europe. He and his wife, Sharon (a mortgage banker who is also a published writer), live in Marble Hill, Missouri, with their dogs and cat. Besides writing, Bill and Sharon are involved in collecting and restoring Camaros.

Linda F. Jarrett writes for the *Webster-Kirkwood Times*, *Commerce Magazine*, and www.ladue-frontenac.patch.com. She has written for The *St. Louis Post Dispatch, Missouri Life, St. Louis Construction News & Review, St. Louis Bride, St. Louis Family, Today's Home*, and *Ladue News.* She coauthored a travel book, *Quick Escapes from St. Louis* for the Globe Pequot Press, has written *Hotels and B&B's* for www.citysearch.com, and has researched and written medical articles for www.CBSnews.com/HealthWatch.

Her website is www.write4y.com.

Jerry-Mac Johnston is the fourth generation of a theatrical family. He has appeared in over 100 plays, television and movies including the popular series *Northern Exposure*. As a writer Jerry-Mac has written children's books, plays and his poetry has been published internationally. His first volume of poetry, *Naked Ladies, Bleacher Seats and A New Denim Jacket*, is set for a 2011 publication. Jerry-Mac physically lives in Springfield, Missouri, but his mind is elsewhere.

Shaun Jordan grew up in Georgia but has called southwest Missouri home for the past decade. He lives with his wife and stepson, and enjoys the winter because he always finds money in the pockets of his coat.

Linda Joyce aspires to be a novelist. She is published in poetry and nonfiction. Recently, her manuscript *Bayou Bound* received first place in the SWA Past President's Romance Award. Poetry is her guilty pleasure. She is the former Vice President of Whispering Prairie Press and Creative Director for Kansas City Literary Magazine. She is also a member of several writing groups, including the Missouri Writers' Guild.

Susan Kirkpatrick was founder and editor of *Ozarks Magazine* and is the author (Susan Croce Kelly) of *Route 66, the highway and its people*, an award-winning history of the old road published by University of Oklahoma Press (with photographer Quinta Scott). She has been a newspaper reporter in Springfield and St. Louis, an award-winning columnist in Texas, public relations executive in St. Louis and Chicago, worked in Belgium and England, and has been president of her own corporate writing business since 1994. Susan has written dozens of freelance articles for newspapers and magazines across the country.

Suzan Klassen, "Suzy," was a young child during this 1960's hailstorm in Hutchinson, Kansas. The events recorded here are true to the best of her memory. An adult for many years now, she lives in the Kansas City area. She and her husband have three almost grown children. She is published in *101 Facets of Faith* and *Focus on Your Child*.

Christopher Limber is a poet, playwright, lyricist and composer. His published works include two plays, *Me and Richard 3* and *Quick Brewed Macbeth*, both of which won the St. Louis Kevin Kline award for *Outstanding Production for Young Audiences*. His published scores include *Kabuki Ugly Duckling* and *The Secret Garden*; both are collaborations with playwright, Pamela Sterling. Mr. Limber is Education Director for Shakespeare Festival St. Louis.

Dave Malone is the author of several books of poetry and a new eBook series, *Seasons in Love* (Trask Road Press), available at Smashwords and Kindle. His poems have appeared in various online and print journals as well. His interests include Ozark culture and crime fiction, and he maintains a web presence at *davemalone.net*.

Deborah Marshall, a former reporter and news editor, now writes historical fiction and creative nonfiction. Her work has been published in newspapers, magazines and anthologies. She is currently working on her second historical fiction novel in her *Yesterday's Ladies* series. Deborah is the 2011-12 president of the Missouri Writers' Guild and founder of the Missouri Warrior Writers Project, which she directs with Kelli Allen. She is a Fellow in the 2012 Regional Arts Commission Community Arts Training (CAT) Institute.

Caryn Mirriam-Goldberg is the 2009-2012 Poet Laureate of Kansas, and a long-time transformative language artist. As a poet, fiction and nonfiction writer, teacher, mentor, and facilitator, she explores and celebrates how the spoken, written and sung word can help us live more meaningful and vibrant lives. Founder of Transformative Language Arts at Goddard College (where she teaches), and facilitator of Brave Voice workshops, she values social and personal transformation through the spoken, written and sung word.

Pierre J. Moeser is a physician who lives in Chesterfield, Missouri, with his wife. He enjoys visiting his children who attend Fordham University in New York and USC in L.A. His passions are writing, sailing, and traveling with his family. He is a member of the St. Louis Writers Guild, the Chesterfield Writers Guild, and SCBWI. Besides his articles in national medical journals, Dr. Moeser has published several short stories and essays.

Claudia Mundell has a Border War in her writing. She grew up in Kansas, but her work life has been in Missouri. She has many memories from each state that work their way into her fiction. After raising a family and teaching, she now writes for pleasure—and maybe for profit someday. Her work has ap-peared in *MidRivers Review, Yellow Medicine Review, Redbud,*

TEA, Good Old Days, Romantic Homes, and others along with several anthologies.

Melina Neet is a writer who lives in Kansas City, whose film criticism has been published in Kansas City and New York periodicals. She is currently researching the life of E.A. Poe for a theatre project for 2012. *Wizard of Oz* is among her favorite films, and she still has a crush on Ray Bolger as the Scarecrow.

DeAnna Quietwater Noriega is half Apache and a quarter Chippewa. She lives in Fulton, Missouri, and works for Services for Independent Living in Columbia as an Independent Living Specialist in blindness and low vision services. She has been a storyteller, writer and poet since childhood.

Niki Nymark is a St. Louis poet. Her work appears in several local, national and international anthologies and she has a chapbook in the Midwestern Women Poets series published by Cherry Pie Press. Her work is often autobiographical and humorous, although Screaming Woman is neither.

Lynn Obermoeller is an author of articles and essays. Lynn resides in St. Louis, Missouri, where she is a member of St. Louis Writers Guild and a member of Saturday Writers.

Michelle O'Brien is a partner and Vice President of Operations at VITEC, Inc. however she continues to act in the familiar capacity of chef and cheerleader because she (secretly) loves it! In the spare time Michelle finds between family, friends and VITEC, she is penning a novel. The enjoyment she derives from writing elicits a Cheshire catlike grin every time. Michelle is a seasoned marketer and contributing author to many websites and business articles.

Linda O'Connell is an award-winning member of St. Louis Writers Guild and Missouri State Poetry Society, On The Edge.

Rosalie O'Leary lives with her partner, and a couple of old dogs, in a new house on five tornado ravaged acres in Southwest Missouri, where she enjoys reading and writing poetry, and watching the birds in the field.

Nancy Peacock is a retired librarian writing from Fort Smith, Arkansas. She loves books, and will read anything. She is a member of River Valley Writers, Ozark Writers League and the Columbia Chapter of the Missouri Writers' Guild. Her husband of fifty-four years, three daughters and their families like to read her stories. She's been published in *Echoes of the Ozarks*, *Cuivre River Anthology*, *Mysteries of the Ozarks* and *Well Versed*.

Shiloh Peters has been a resident of the state of Missouri since birth and is thus, a fellow sufferer of volatile Midwestern weather. She is currently studying for a Masters of English at Missouri State University in Springfield.

Von Pittman has worked in the field of distance education at Washington State University and the Universities of Georgia, Iowa, and Missouri. In addition to academic writing, he authored the self-help book, *Surviving Graduate School Part-Time*. His fiction has appeared in the periodicals *Well Versed* and *The Study Guide*, and the anthology, *Diamonds in the Rough*. His story "Covering the Spread" won the 2008 Short Story Award of the Missouri Writers' Guild.

Cynthia Reeg, Midwest born and raised, based this story on a real life event in her father's life. Cynthia's writings have appeared in numerous children's magazines. Her picture book series, *The Pet Grammar Parade* and *Gifts from God* are available from Guardian Angel Publishing. Her story, "The Emily Explosion" is part of *The Girls*, available from Blooming Tree Press. For more information visit www.cynthiareeg.com

Linda Neal Reising has been published in *The Southern Indiana Review, Comstock Review, Open 24 Hours*, and *Fruitflesh: Seeds of Inspiration for Women Who Write*, by HarperCollins. She was named first place winner in the 2009 Judith Siegel Pearson Writing Award. Her award-winning poem and short story were published in *Lost on Route 66, Tales of the Mother Road*. Linda's book *Women at Forty* was named a finalist in the "Pathways" International Poetry Contest for Women.

Shirley Rickett has numerous published poems to her credit. Once a resident of Kansas City, she now resides in the Rio Grande Valley.

Bev Rohlf is a retired music educator, principal, and fine arts coordinator for a public school system in Missouri. She is currently pursuing the university study of literature and writing.

Howard Simms was a retired employee of Pittsburgh Plate Glass factory. He married his childhood sweetheart, Verna Hill, in 1940 and together they raised two daughters, Dolores and Jeannette. At the time of his death in 2007, the couple had celebrated sixty-six years of happy married life. Verna is donating his story as a memory to Howard and knows he would be pleased to help the children of Joplin in this small way.

Jordan Smith is currently a senior English Education major at Culver-Stockton College, Canton, Missouri. She has been published in *Harmony,* Culver-Stockton's literary and art magazine. She intends to teach middle and high school English while ever continuing her education in pursuit of eventual Master and Doctorial degrees.

Bonnie Stepenoff is a professor of history at Southeast Missouri State University in Cape Girardeau, Missouri. She is the author of five nonfiction books, including *The Dead End Kids of St. Louis: Homeless Boys and the People Who Tried to Save Them* (University of Missouri Press, 2010), and many articles. Her poetry has been published in *Modern Haiku, Frogpond, the Heron's Nest, Bellowing Ark,* and other journals.

Phillip Ronald Stormer is an associate professor of English at Culver-Stockton College in Canton, Missouri. In addition to teaching literature courses, he teaches Introduction to Creative Writing, Fiction Workshop, and Poetry Workshop.

Susan Swartwout is Professor of creative writing and publishing at Southeast Missouri State University and is the Publisher of Southeast Missouri State University Press which produces full-length books, three annual writing contests, and *Big Muddy: Journal of the Mississippi River Valley,* an interdisciplinary magazine. Her two collections of poetry are entitled *Freaks* and *Uncommon Ground,* she co-edited *Real Things: Anthology of Popular Culture in American Poetry, Hurricane Blues: Poems about Katrina and Rita, Balancing on a Bootheel,* and *A Student's Guide to Getting Published.* Her poems and short stories are published in literary journals such as *Nebraska Review, The Laurel Review, River Styx, Negative*

Capability, Mississippi Review, and *Spoon River Poetry Review,* among others. She is a recipient of the Rona Jaffe Writers' Foundation Award, the Dillinger Good Award, and St. Louis Poetry Center's Hanks Award.

Bonnie K. Tesh, originally from Joplin, currently resides on Table Rock Lake. She is coauthor of the inspirational book, *I'll Push, You Steer; the Definitive Guide to Stumbling Through Life with Blinders on.* She has won numerous awards for her short stories and essays.

Anene M. Tressler-Hauschultz is an Emmy-award winning writer who resides in Kirkwood, Missouri. Her debut novel, *Dancing With Gravity* (written under the pen name, Anene Tressler) was published in March 2011 by Blank Slate Press. The novel has been awarded first prize for literary fiction in the 2011 International Book Awards. She is a member of the St. Louis and Missouri Writers' Guilds.

Susan Varno has published over 100 articles about Ozarks people and history. These include feature articles for the Three Rivers Edition of the *Arkansas Democrat Gazette* and a history column in the *White River Current* Newspaper. Since 1989, she has written monthly columns and movie reviews for *Video Views* Magazine. Twenty-two of her short stories have been published in confession and other magazines. She is the newsletter editor for Twin Lakes Writers, Mountain Home, Arkansas.

Roberta Vaughan Schwinke lives in rural Osage County, Missouri, near the little village of Fredericksburg. She enjoys writing poetry and history. She works at the county Historical Society, where she gets much of the inspiration for her stories.

She has had several poems and short essays published in the *Ozarks Mountaineer* and other magazines. She also has a story in the recently published *Mysteries of the Ozarks*. She is now at work on a "deep" history of Fredericksburg.

Elaine Viets writes two bestselling mystery series, the *Dead-End Job Mysteries* and the *Josie Marcus Mystery Shopper Mysteries*. She was a newspaper columnist in St. Louis for over twenty-five years and now lives in Ft. Lauderdale, Florida.

Gloria Vando's latest book, *Shadows & Supposes* (Arte Público Press), won the Poetry Society of America's Di Castagnola Award and the Latino Literary Hall of Fame's Poetry Book Award. Her poems have appeared in magazines, anthologies, and on the Grammy-nominated *Poetry on Record: 98 Poets Read Their Work 1888-2006*. She is founder of Helicon Nine Editions, which received the Governor's Arts Award (KS), and cofounder of The Writers Place, a literary center in Kansas City.

Donna Volkenannt's love for stories began when her mother read to her *The Little Engine That Could*. Donna still favors stories with inspiring characters who overcome hardships. The real-life characters who inspire her are her husband and their grandchildren, who all live together in St. Peters, Missouri. She believes that despite occasional stormy weather, the Show Me State is a wonderful place to live—especially for writers. Learn more about Donna on her blog donnasbookpub.blogspot.com

Pat Wahler is a freelance writer from St. Peters, Missouri. She has published stories in multiple anthologies including *Chicken Soup for the Dog Lover's Soul* and *Cup of Comfort for Cat*

*Lover*s. She blogs all things animals at Critter Alley, www.critteralley.blogspot.com.

Student Authors

Ryan Burks, son of Michael and Dawn Burks, loves playing baseball and being out in the wild.

Victoria Fishback, daughter of Rick and Ashley Fishback, plays on the Fair Grove volleyball team and is very athletic.

Hannah Fox, daughter of Cathy and Alan Fox, likes to be with friends, write, and listen to music.

Hannah Mallard, daughter of Ken and Erin Mallard, loves to play volleyball and loves cheerleading. She also has a heart for animals and people that need help.

Cody Sisco, son of Tim and Kelly Sisco, loves sports and the outdoors. In his spare time, he can be found out in the woods or with a glove and ball.

Leah Wahlquist, daughter of Eric and Michelle Wahlquist, enjoys playing volleyball and writing. When she grows up, she wants to be a nurse, a doctor, or an interior designer. Leah is in several extracurricular activities including volleyball, cheerleading, Honor Choir, and reading groups. She is also a Middle School Ambassador.

www.ingramcontent.com/pod-product-compliance
Lightning Source LLC
Chambersburg PA
CBHW051514170626
46811CB00002B/826